Far from Gringo Land

Far from Gringo Land

Edward Myers

CLARION BOOKS
Houghton Mifflin Harcourt
Boston · New York
2009

Copyright © 2009 by Edward Myers

The text was set in 12-point Bembo.
Book designed by Kerry Martin

For information about permission to reproduce selections from this book, write to
Permissions, Houghton Mifflin Harcourt Publishing Company,
215 Park Avenue South, New York, New York 10003.

Clarion Books is an imprint of Houghton Mifflin Harcourt Publishing Company.
www.hmhbooks.com
Manufactured in the United States of America

Library of Congress Cataloging-in-Publication Data
Myers, Edward, 1950–
Far from gringo land / by Edward Myers.
p. cm.
Summary: In the barrio of Santo Domingo, Mexico, seventeen-year-old Rick Dresner
of Colorado helps family friends build a new house while learning much about
poverty, hospitality, pride, and living as a member of the minority.
ISBN 978-0-547-05630-2
[1. Building—Fiction. 2. Interpersonal relations—Fiction. 3. Americans—Mexico—Fiction.
4. Family life—Mexico—Fiction. 5. Mexico—Fiction.] I. Title.
PZ7.M98255Far 2009
[Fic]—dc22
2009015828

MP 10 9 8 7 6 5 4 3 2 1

To the Rivera family—
Con mucho cariño—E.M.

Special thanks to

Carol Gaskin

Marcia Leonard

Delia Marshall

Cory Myers

Robin Myers

Noé Orozco S.

Alejandra Ortíz de Rivera

Edith Poor

Jesús Rivera Juárez

José Rivera Ortíz

Amy Shapiro

Dinah Stevenson

Far from
Gringo Land

I

Arrival

Seated on a bench in the *jardín público,* the town square in the center of Santo Domingo, Rick Dresner shivers slightly in the early morning chill. He's alone. His backpack and roll-aboard are at his feet. He didn't sleep much during the two-day journey here, but even so, he feels wide awake. Everything is different from home— the ancient buildings, the flowery scent in the air, the sound of the birds calling to one another from the trees around him—and that gives him energy despite his exhaustion. Now a rhythmic gong catches his attention—the town clock tolling six times. The birds fall silent for a moment, then jolt upward, dozens at once, flying off with a great windy noise.

The town starts to wake up. A hunched-over old man sweeps a sidewalk with a long-handled broom. Shopkeepers arrive and unlock the doors to their shops. Three schoolboys run by. A waiter sets up tables at an outdoor café. Rick watches these activities and decides he'd better get moving, too.

Following directions he'd received in the mail, he heads up a steep street. White walls flank it, and stone doorways with massive wooden doors appear on both sides at regular intervals. The windows, too, are framed in stone, some covered with complex iron grilles. Breathing hard, burdened by the backpack and roll-aboard, Rick forces his way upward.

At some point he stops to rest, turns, and finds Santo Domingo spread out before him. The roofs are mostly flat, gray concrete, though here and there he sees a few expanses of red tile. Dark green trees rise between some of the buildings. The reddish-yellow bell towers of six or eight churches rise over everything else. This is the view that appears in so many photos and postcards of the town. Yet Rick sees it in another way, too—as a memory he can't quite place.

He sets off again.

Once the hill levels off, the street opens up into an unpaved area with houses surrounding it on three of the four sides. The fourth side is an overlook that lets Rick gaze down on some cultivated fields, several tile-roofed adobe houses, the ruins of an old aqueduct, and the gray-green desert beyond. This, too, is a half-remembered view. He stares, trying to fill in the blanks in his memory. The last time he saw this landscape was ten years ago, when he was seven. He turns away. Surrounding him is a barrio, a neighborhood that's the poorest he's seen all morning. Rough brick walls. Clay tile roofs. Clotheslines full of dangling laundry that crisscross between houses—some of them little more than shacks. A thin haze of wood smoke lingers over the area. Three or four radios blare music from different stations.

Rick finds the entrance to a street that's only five or six feet wide. Callejón Hidalgo, reads a tile plaque mounted on the wall. Hidalgo Alley. It's so narrow that even the thought of entering it makes Rick feel claustrophobic. He glances around. Two little girls and a woman stare at him from a second-story window across the street.

"*¡Hola, gringo!*" calls one of the girls.

Rick knows that "*gringo*" is often considered an insulting

term for an American, but he doesn't think she intended it that way. She was smiling as she called out to him.

"*Hola,*" he calls back.

The girls giggle. The woman, her long black braids dangling as she leans out the window, simply stares.

"*Busco la familia Romero,*" Rick says to her. I'm looking for the Romero family.

"*No los conozco,*" replies the woman. I don't know them.

Rick thanks her anyway and starts up Callejón Hidalgo. The cobbled surface is uneven underfoot. He has to carry the roll-aboard and steps carefully to avoid twisting an ankle. The walls are too close for comfort, and the street's narrowness leaves it cool and gloomy. For a moment he feels a twinge of worry. Maybe this isn't such a great place for a lone gringo. But the numbers painted on the whitewashed walls and doorways keep increasing, so he knows he's getting closer to his destination. Eight, ten, eleven, thirteen, fourteen . . .

At the corner, where Callejón Hidalgo widens to meet Callejón Catarata, he finds number seventeen.

Setting down the roll-aboard, Rick hesitates for a moment. Finally, he pulls a knotted rope dangling from a hole in the door. A bell clanks somewhere on the other side.

The second he hears it, a string of thoughts flashes through his brain: *What am I doing here? Why am I visiting this strange place . . . moving in with people I barely know . . . taking on a job I've never done before?* Panic surges through his body, leaving him weak and shaky. He fights the impulse to flee. To head back through Callejón Hidalgo, race down to the *jardín público,* and catch the first bus out. To return to Mexico City, fly back to Colorado, and make up a story to tell his parents.

The door swings open.

On the other side stands a man clearly much older than Rick, but almost a head shorter.

"*Busco los Romeros,*" Rick tells him. I'm looking for the Romeros.

"*¿Eres Ricardo?*" the man asks. Are you Richard? He smiles warmly, and Rick glimpses a gold-framed front tooth.

"*Sí—Rick Dresner.*"

"*Yo soy Julio Romero,*" says the man. I am Julio Romero. He opens his arms and gives Rick a hug. "*Estás en tu casa.*" You're in your house. He picks up Rick's bag and leads him through a narrow entryway into a rather plain-looking kitchen, then down some stairs into a courtyard.

Suddenly two little dogs are jumping and yapping at Rick, a large woman is embracing him, a young man is shaking his hand, and everyone is speaking at once.

"*—y que hayas tenido buen viaje—*"

"*—y llegaste sin problema!*"

"*—bienvenido.*"

The sounds swirl around Rick until he's dizzy. He recognizes the Spanish words but can't make sense of them. Still, the intention is clear: he's welcome here. Although he barely remembers these people—Julio, Emiliana, and Francisco—he's among friends.

The Romeros

Early that afternoon, they sit down to a big meal. Emiliana has prepared lentil soup, rice, beans, and chicken in a fluffy tomato sauce. There's bread, too, and tortillas heated on a griddle. "Eat," she tells Rick. She gestures with both hands, a brushing motion, and urges him on, using words that he can't quite follow. He catches one phrase, *"muriendo de hambre"*—dying of hunger. She's right about that. He's starving, and this meal is just what he needs. Emiliana serves him second helpings of each dish, then thirds, and he devours everything.

Julio chuckles at Rick's eagerness. "Don't they feed you back home?" he asks. Then he adds, "Welcome to Mexico! We'll show you how to eat."

Though he's almost fifty, Julio's close-cut hair is pure black, and he's slim and muscular. The corners of his mouth droop slightly, so his smile is both a grimace and a smirk.

"Pues, ¿cómo está tu familia?" asks Emiliana. So, how's your family?

"Bien. Completamente bien," Rick answers. Fine. Totally fine.

"That's good," says Emiliana. "I'm happy they're doing so well."

She's about the same age as her husband, but plumpness smoothes her skin, so her face lacks wrinkles. She wears her hair in braids that extend halfway down her back. Her expression is gentle and solemn—until she smiles, revealing a gap-toothed grin that makes Rick smile in return.

"Your parents don't mind sharing you with us?" Francisco asks.

He's Rick's age—seventeen—but looks older. His size is one reason. Although the two of them are the same height, Francisco is stockier, with broad shoulders and a deep chest. His wispy mustache also adds a couple of years to his appearance.

"I miss your mother," says Emiliana. "I wish she could be here, too."

"I'm sure she'd love to visit you," Rick tells her, hoping he's using the right Spanish words. He knows that his mom and Emiliana were close during the families' time together ten years ago and that she's enjoyed the letters they've traded since then. "Maybe when the house is done," he adds.

"*Ojalá,*" she says. I hope so.

The Romeros are strangers, yet they have a place in Rick's life. They're unfamiliar, yet now and then images surface in his memory . . . sitting in a kitchen with a woman who looks like Emiliana, only younger . . . playing near a wall with someone who resembles Francisco, though at age seven instead of seventeen . . . hiking on a hillside with a man who appears to be Julio but seems oddly taller than he is now. Rick takes these bits of recollection and tries to assemble them, but the images come and go like parts of a half-remembered dream.

Much of what he recalls is actually what his parents have told him. That when he was seven, the family drove from Colorado to Mexico and lived for three months in Santo Domingo. That the big old house they'd rented wasn't empty when they arrived, as it should have been, but was still inhabited by the Mexican family working as caretakers for the owner. That Rick's parents invited this family, the Romeros, to stay on during their rental. That the two families became friends and remained in touch long after the Dresners returned to Colorado.

"We're so glad you're here," Emiliana says, jolting Rick from his reverie.

"So am I," Rick replies, feeling more relaxed and excited now. "It's going to be a big adventure."

La Obra

This is the plan. Rick will spend his summer vacation with the Romeros. They'll feed him, give him a place to sleep, introduce him to their way of life, show him Santo Domingo and the surrounding area, and teach him as much Spanish as he can learn in three months. In exchange, he'll help them with *la obra*—the construction project.

The two families have discussed the possibility of this arrangement for a long time, but only recently did it become a real option. It's not that Rick was nervous about leaving home or his parents. He's traveled on his own before. And it's not that he was worried about dealing with another language and culture. He's studied Spanish since junior high. The issue is the difficulty and complexity of *la obra*. Until this year, he wasn't strong enough and big enough to help out.

For the Romeros, *la obra* means building a brick and concrete house. Currently, they live in three tiny rooms. Julio and Emiliana sleep in the bedroom. Francisco sleeps on a sofa in the living room. The other room is a simple kitchen with two tables, a pair of tabletop gas burners, some shelves, an old refrigerator, and a water tank. The rooms stand apart from one another, each set in a corner of the property, facing the irregularly shaped courtyard. All three rooms are cramped, dark, and drafty. The living room has a flat concrete lid; the bedroom and kitchen are roofed with reddish clay tiles. According to Julio, the kitchen roof leaks when it rains. Emiliana's health suffers as a result, and everyone is frustrated by the lack of space.

For years the Romeros have dreamed of building a larger house on their property. Know-how wasn't the problem. Julio, trained as a brick mason, could do most of the work himself, and Francisco could serve as his assistant. The problem was paying for materials. It took the family a long time to save enough money for the bricks and mortar needed to make their dream a reality. Now they have the cash in hand. Rick has arrived to help. Everything is ready.

To show Rick the property and how they intend to change it, Julio and Francisco take him outside and up a wooden ladder to the living room roof. The two little dogs, Tizón and Sombra—Charcoal and Shadow, as Rick has learned—bark as he and the Romeros leave them behind.

The view from the concrete rooftop isn't what Rick expected. He thinks of a house, whether big or small, as one structure, but this house is separate little units within a compound. The three rooms and the boxy walls surrounding them create a cozy haven in the middle. Although small and surfaced with concrete, this central courtyard, *el patio*, is like an oasis. A *pirul*—a big tree with tiny clustered leaves and feathery pink blossoms—provides some shade. Large clay pots of geraniums add splotches of red and a spicy aroma. The expanse of sky overhead makes the place feel surprisingly open. Rick understands why the Romeros feel cramped by the small rooms, but the property, tucked against the hillside, is airy and attractive.

Belatedly, he realizes that Julio is speaking to him.

"*—y aquí mero el colado.*" And right here the—

Rick doesn't know what a *colado* is. Before he can ask, though, Julio turns to him and says, "So what do you think?"

Rick's mind is awash with questions. Where will the new house fit on this small property? Where will the Romeros store all the construction materials? What sequence of steps will they follow in the building process? Unfortunately, he doesn't have a clue how to ask these questions. Despite his years of studying Spanish, he lacks the vocabulary to discuss the construction project. Won't this be a big problem? How can he help build a house if he can't even talk about it? Unsure of what else to say, he answers Julio's question. *"Está bien."* It's fine.

"Are you sure you're ready for this?" Francisco asks seriously.

Rick is overwhelmed by another wave of questions. *Is* he ready? He doesn't really know. And the Romeros—are they doubting his sincerity? His ability to do the work? Or is there some other challenge, some problem with the project that no one has explained? His misgivings flare up again. But what can he say? It's too late to chicken out. More to the point, he really wants to take part in *la obra*. Being in Mexico feels exotic and exciting. He hasn't ever tackled a job as ambitious as this. And best of all, it's nothing like the tough academic work he'll have to do in his final year in high school.

"Of course I'm ready," he says, as much to convince himself as the Romeros.

"It's going to be difficult," Julio says.

"I know."

"We're going to work like mules," Francisco says.

"I know that, too."

They stand for a moment without speaking. To distract himself from the thoughts buzzing in his head, Rick walks a few paces toward the roof's edge, pretending that something has caught his attention. At once something does—the view. It's the same view of Santo Domingo that he saw earlier, but he's much higher up the hillside now, so the panorama is wider. The land drops away below him, and he gazes at the roofs, the treetops, the church towers, and the town square from the perspective of someone looking out of a low-flying plane. The desert beyond the town rolls away toward the horizon.

Everything shimmers in the summer heat, blurring the edges of the view so that Santo Domingo seems to be an island suspended in the middle of nowhere. Rick suddenly feels disconnected from the rest of the world—and from time as well. In this place, with half-familiar people standing nearby and odd sounds welling up from the vista below, his past—growing up in Colorado, living with his parents, going to an American high school—seems as dreamlike as the desert landscape in the distance.

Good Night

"*Buenas noches,*" Francisco says that evening as the boys settle into their beds. Francisco will sleep on a mattress on the floor; Rick has inherited the sofa.

"*Buenas noches,*" Rick replies. As an only child, he has always had a bedroom to himself. Will he have trouble sleeping with someone nearby? He pulls up the covers and sinks into the cushions as if submerging in water. Down, down, down . . .

An image flits through his mind: his parents saying goodbye to him at the Denver airport. He knows they're happy that he's making this trip, but they were more upset by his departure than he'd expected. Embarrassed by their emotional farewell—his mother crying, his dad all choked up—he'd entered the security clearance area with a sense of relief.

Only one more year till I leave for college, he thinks. He can hardly wait. He loves his parents, but he's tired of living at home. He wants to explore the world, to have adventures. Now, at least, he's made a start.

Mexico, he tells himself. *I'm in Mexico.*

He thinks about his bedroom back in Denver—large, quiet, and entirely his own—and feels a twinge of homesickness. "We love you," his dad had called out after Rick had given his boarding pass and ID to the agent. He'd meant to call back, "I love you, too," but the line of passengers had already advanced far enough through security that all he could do was turn and wave goodbye. Had he hurt his parents' feelings?

Rick is beyond tired. All he wants is seven or eight hours of sleep. He needs to be well rested. Julio intends to start *la obra* tomorrow.

Everything will work out, he tells himself. *Everything will be fine.*

Fatigue finally overtakes him. He sinks into oblivion.

You Like Mexican Work?

Early the next morning, Rick rolls off the couch and dresses quickly in a T-shirt, a long-sleeved shirt, jeans, and work boots.

Emiliana greets him warmly when he enters the kitchen. She's wearing a flowered apron over an almost shapeless cotton dress. "I hope you slept well," she says.

"Very well, thanks," Rick tells her, still feeling somewhat dazed. Then, in case he didn't sound convincing enough, he adds cheerily, "I feel great!"

At that moment, Julio comes in. He's dressed in tan jeans, a plaid western-style shirt, and a sombrero about the size and shape of an American cowboy hat. *"Buenos días, Ricardo,"* he says, taking off his hat and sitting at the kitchen table.

"Buenos días."

"Ya llegó la arena." The sand has arrived.

"What sand?" Rick asks, puzzled.

"The big load I ordered. We'll use it for making *mezcla.*"

Rick isn't sure what *mezcla* is. He knows that *mezclar* means "to mix," so *mezcla* must be some sort of mixed construction material. Concrete, maybe? He guesses at the Spanish word by using the risky method of adding *o* to the English. *"Concreto?"*

"No," Julio replies. *"Mezcla."*

Rick decides not to press the point. He'll find out soon enough.

Stepping outside after breakfast, Rick expects to see a big pile of sand by the Romeros' door. There's nothing there. The open area where Callejón Hidalgo intersects Callejón Catarata is completely empty. "Where is it?" he asks Julio.

Julio motions toward Hidalgo. They head down the alley without speaking. It's barely seven o'clock. Rick can hear families talking in the houses right and left, and he smells fried food—breakfast cooking. A few people are out, mostly men in jean jackets and sombreros, and some of them nod to Julio in passing. Otherwise the *callejón* is empty. Chilly, too. Its walls are so high that they block the sun's rays at this early hour. Rick stretches out his arms and discovers that he can nearly touch both walls with his hands.

That's what brings the situation home. The alley is much too narrow for a truck. Even a car wouldn't make it through. The heap of sand that Rick first imagined sitting outside the Romeros' house is a block away.

Julio and Rick reach the end of the *callejón*. Just to the left, dumped against a brick wall, is a beige mound at least five feet tall, ten feet wide, and ten feet deep.

Julio whistles through his teeth in amazement—or maybe dismay.

"How much do you think it weighs?" Rick asks.

"I ordered several tons." Julio chuckles quietly.

Rick begins to understand the task ahead of them. Several tons . . . Three? Four? *Metric* tons, yet: 1,000 kilograms per ton, or 2,200 pounds. The Romeros' house is a full block away. Using wheelbarrows to move this huge pile of sand would be best, but the *callejón* is bumpy, muddy, and slick. There's also a drainage trench about six inches wide running down the center for several hundred feet. A wheelbarrow would be tough to control. Maybe even impossible.

"How do we do this?" Rick asks uneasily, wondering, *Can it even be done?*

The answer: *"Costales."* Another word Rick doesn't recognize.

They go back to the house, and Julio shows Rick a little pile of neatly folded coarse cloth bags. Each bag will hold about 25 kilos of sand, Julio says. Rick does some quick multiplication. At 2.2 pounds per kilo, that's 55 pounds of sand in each *costal*.

"But where do you put them?" he asks Julio.

Francisco, who has just finished breakfast, joins them at that moment. He has heard Rick's question and looks puzzled. "Put what?"

"The sacks of sand," Rick says.

Julio and Francisco exchange glances. "Well—on our backs," says Julio.

The morning heats up. Direct sunlight won't enter the steep alley for several hours, but the air grows gradually warmer. Rick's muscles warm up, too; soon he's limber. For the next hour, he proceeds without major problems. He loads his *costal* with sand, hoists it onto his back, and carries it carefully up Callejón Hidalgo. Passing through the Romeros' kitchen, he descends the staircase into the courtyard and dumps his load onto the growing pile there. Then he repeats the process. Sometimes his efforts are synchronized with Julio's or Francisco's; sometimes he works alone. Slowly, slowly, the pile on the corner diminishes. Slowly, slowly, the pile in the courtyard grows larger. Still, he finds it hard to believe that he won't be hauling sand until the end of time.

The sun clears the rooftops; the day grows hot. Rick strips off his shirt, but his T-shirt is quickly drenched in sweat. His hands keep slipping, so he can't keep a good grip on the sacks.

How many trips has he made? Thirty? Forty? He lost track hours ago. Three dozen trips at least, he assures himself, maybe more. Soon he's too tired to care.

He notices that some men have shown up and are hanging out on a pile of big rocks a short distance from the sand. There must be eight or nine of them. Some are middle-aged, others are younger, a few are teenagers. They're talking and laughing. They're also clearly watching Rick, Julio, and Francisco struggle with the sand. Rick doesn't want to pay too much attention; he's self-conscious enough as it is. When Julio and Francisco are with him, the situation isn't so bad. Once they head off with their loads, though, Rick can hear the voices grow louder, the laughter increase, and the tone of the comments change.

"¡Oye, gringo!" someone shouts.

Rick pretends not to hear. He keeps shoveling sand into the costal.

"¡Gringo!"

He waves but otherwise ignores the taunt.

"Tú—¿eres sordo?" You—are you deaf?

Rick glances down Hidalgo, wondering how soon Francisco or Julio will return. He decides that ignoring the men will only make things worse. He turns to them, gives them a mock salute, and calls out, *"¿Qué tal, señores?"* How's it going, gentlemen?

That silences everyone for a moment. A few comments follow, then a flurry of laughs.

Rick wonders what's setting them off. Do they think it's funny to see him—a stranger—working so hard? Are they mocking him because he's an American? He's both embarrassed and annoyed by their taunts. This isn't the response he expected. He thought the people in the Romeros' neighborhood might be impressed that he's working side by side with Julio and Francisco. He thought people might even—who knows—*respect* him. Instead, they seem to be making him the butt of their jokes.

Finished filling the *costal,* Rick squats, pushes it against his back, and forces himself upright. His left boot skitters on the ground, throwing him off balance. He lurches, struggling to keep a hold on the *costal,* then manages to stand. The load makes his back and shoulders ache, but he's determined to stay upright. Anything to avoid humiliating himself.

The men applaud, cheer, and whistle loudly. *"Oye, gringo— ¿te gusta el trabajo mexicano?"* one of them yells. You like Mexican work?

The truth is, Rick hates this work! He's exhausted and sore. He's dripping with sweat. All he wants is to stagger back to the house and collapse on the couch. But that isn't a choice. It would be giving in to these guys' mockery. It would be letting down the Romeros.

"I'm glad to be helping my friends," Rick answers stiffly in Spanish; then he trudges up the alley.

R and R

And so *la obra* begins. Starting early each day, when the air is still fairly cool, they undertake their construction tasks. One morning, they visit a friend of Julio's to borrow four shovels, a garden hose, a stack of square metal buckets called *botes,* and a bag of tools for laying concrete. Then they carry all of these items back home through the winding streets of Santo Domingo. Then, for two days, they haul a ton of *grava*—big chunks of crushed rock for making concrete—from the far end of Callejón Hidalgo to the house. The day after that, they haul four dozen bags of cement—each weighing almost seventy pounds—the same distance. Every day it's something different. Julio, Francisco, and Rick do most of the manual labor. Emiliana does some, too, but mostly she keeps the household running. By one or two o'clock each afternoon, as the day heats up and everyone grows weary, they sit down to a big midday meal she has prepared.

Rick feels more exhausted than at any other time in his life. His muscles are sore to the touch. His whole body quivers with fatigue. Has he ever really *worked* before, he wonders—ever in his entire life? Nothing compares to the effort he's making now. Not the supermarket stock-boy job. Not the lawn-mowing job.

Certainly not the library job. And school, by comparison, has been like a day at a country club. Somehow he never thought *la obra* would be so tough. He never expected the construction tasks to be so—so *awful*. To prepare for the trip, he spent more time at the school gym than usual. But all the aerobic workouts and weight training didn't do much to prepare him for what he's doing now. He wants to lie down and sleep for a week.

The food Emiliana serves at the midday meal offers some comfort. Homemade vegetable soup, pork chops in a spicy sauce, yellow squash, beans jumbled together with rice, fat little cheese-stuffed tortillas, and, for dessert, a yellow custard called *flan*. It's as much food as Rick would ordinarily eat in a day. He accepts the offer of seconds. He goes along with thirds. Devouring all this food definitely helps; he's still tired after eating, but he doesn't feel as weak.

One day, after a welcome *siesta*—the first afternoon nap that Rick has taken in years—Julio announces that they're all going down to *el centro,* Santo Domingo's historic town center.

"An errand?" Rick inquires.

"Un paseo," replies Francisco. A stroll.

Rick isn't sure that a stroll is what his body needs right now. But he figures if this is what counts as R and R in small-town Mexico, he'd better grab the chance.

They all set off. After a ten- or fifteen-minute walk, they reach the *jardín público,* the plaza where Rick sat for a while on his first day in Santo Domingo. Surrounded by cafés, hotels, art galleries, and shops selling antiques, jewelry, and Mexican crafts, the *jardín* is about half a block square, with staircases at the corners leading upward to a parklike area. Trees and plants along the edges filter some of the noise from cars, radios, and street vendors. There's a bandstand at the center and benches set up all around it. Inside this little haven, people sit and rest, sip soft drinks, read newspapers, eat ice cream, or simply watch the tide of people drifting by. Mexican moms with kids. American and European tourists. Local businessmen chatting over coffee. Vendors selling balloons, candy, lottery tickets, magazines, and souvenirs. A few beggars, mostly barefoot kids.

"You like it?" Francisco asks.

"Very much," Rick replies.

Looking around, Julio spots an empty bench and claims it. The others follow. Rick grunts in pain when he sits.

Julio notices. "Are you all right?"

"Fine. Just a little sore."

"I hope we're not pushing you too hard," says Emiliana.

"No, I'm fine. Really," he reassures them quickly. But he wonders, *How can they look so relaxed and rested? Am I the only one who's totally beat?*

"Something to drink?" Francisco asks.

"Maybe later."

They fall silent, simply enjoying the shade and the sight of all the people hanging out in the *jardín público*.

Watching, Rick realizes that while most of them are Mexicans, plenty are Americans. He hears English almost as often as Spanish. "I still think you could have gotten a better price," says a frizzy-haired woman on a nearby bench. From somewhere else in the park a boy shouts, "I wanted the *green* balloon!" The mood is festive. Everyone seems to be getting along. But Rick notices that Americans seem to hang out only with Americans, Mexicans only with Mexicans. The few interactions between the two nationalities occur when the vendors approach the tourists. Otherwise the members of each group keep almost entirely to themselves.

A family of Americans wanders past, catching Rick's attention: a father with three girls, all pretty. The oldest, a redhead dressed in jeans and a light green T-shirt, looks about his age. She turns abruptly, gazes back at him, and smiles.

"Jeez, that was such a laugh!" one of the younger girls is saying. At once the redhead turns away. In a few moments the family is gone.

What caught her attention? Rick wonders. Was she staring because she liked his looks? Or only because she noticed he was hanging out with Mexicans? Did she find him appealing—or just puzzling?

None of the Romeros comments, though Francisco, turning to Rick, raises one eyebrow and smiles.

Rick gazes across the *jardín,* trying to spot the redhead and her family. If he were alone, he could have gotten up, kept them in sight, and maybe figured out a way to bump into them again. Even talk to them. Hanging out with the Romeros, though, he can't break away.

At that moment he feels a longing that's a bit like homesickness, only stronger.

Long Distance

"So, anyway," Rick says toward the end of his first phone call home, "that's about it." He has told his parents about his trip, about his first week in Santo Domingo, about settling in, about *la obra*. He has passed on the Romeros' greetings and good wishes. He has answered his parents' questions about how the Romeros are doing. He has assured them he's fine. Now, standing in a booth at the Teléfonos de México office in *el centro,* he grows restless.

"It sounds as if you're off to a terrific start," Dad says.

"We're glad everything has gone so well," Mom says.

Rick can't think of anything to reply. He imagines them at home: Dad on the phone in the study, Mom on the extension in the master bedroom. He can't shake the feeling that his parents miss him more than he misses them, that they want more from him—more news, more emotion, more something—than he can give them. Feeling both awkward and resentful, he finally breaks the silence.

"Sorry," he says. "I'd better go."

"Sure," Dad says.

"We know you're busy," Mom says.

He feels a pang of love for them but doesn't know how to express it. "Thanks for everything," he says. "I'll call you again soon."

Relatives

Several of the Romeros' relatives live in the neighborhood, and Rick meets them as the days pass. Emiliana's sister, Carmen, has a house just down the hill, and she stops by now and then to say hello. She's a cheerful woman, about forty, whose squat face, wide smile, and somewhat bulging eyes give her more than a passing resemblance to a frog. Rick likes her a lot; she's friendly, relaxed, and easy to talk with.

There's also Aniseto, the oldest of Julio's five older brothers. Skinny and frail, he looks to be seventy-five or eighty, but, Rick is shocked to learn, he's actually just sixty-three. Chronic poor health and a hard life have aged him. Because he walks with some difficulty, Aniseto doesn't visit the Romeros very often. When he does, conversations are brief. He is cordial but somber, as if trapped in the cage of his illnesses.

Rick has learned that another of Julio's brothers, Juan, lives nearby with his family—in fact, right next door. But despite the physical closeness, Rick hasn't met Juan or his wife, Antonia, or any of their children.

Then one morning, a little girl in a dirty cotton dress and plastic sandals shows up at the house. She looks five or six but turns out to be eight. Skinny and stick-legged, she is tiny but pretty, with a head of curly black hair and the darkest eyes that Rick has ever seen. She stares at him a long time without blinking.

"Ricardo, this is Hilaria, my niece," Emiliana announces. "Hilaria, this is señor Dresner."

The child's gaze is so intense that Rick quickly grows uncomfortable.

"Hola, gringuito," she finally says in a singsong voice. Hi, little gringo.

Rick smiles. *Little* gringo? Hilaria is almost ten years younger than he is and about one-third his size. *"Hola,"* he replies. *"¿Cómo estás?"*

"Bien, gringuito. ¿Y cómo estás tú?" Fine, little gringo. And how are you?

"Fine."

"Where are you from, little gringo?"

Rick decides to make a joke. "I come from Gringolandia."

She giggles. "Gringolandia. Is that far away?"

"Very far."

"Are there lots of gringos there?"

"Lots and lots," he says, "though not as many as here."

Julio, Francisco, and Emiliana chuckle at this wisecrack.

"And why are *you* here, little gringo?" asks Hilaria.

"I'm visiting your aunt, uncle, and cousin," he replies.

"Don't you like it back in Gringolandia?"

"I do," Rick tells her, "but I like it here, too."

This answer seems to satisfy the girl. But just as Rick thinks he's off the hook, she asks, "Are you very rich, little gringo?"

He can't help laughing. "Me? No way!"

No one else laughs.

Immediately, Rick sees the absurdity of his words. Of *course* he's rich. By comparison with the people here, how could he *not* be rich? He blushes.

Emiliana sees Rick's discomfort and speaks up. "Hilaria is my helper," she says. "She usually comes here twice a week."

"I'm sure she's a very fine helper," Rick replies, unsure what else to say.

"*Gracias, gringuito,*" says Hilaria, clearly pleased.

Pets

The Romeros' yappy dogs, Tizón and Sombra, are pets in one sense—animals kept out of affection and for enjoyment. But they also have a job: warding off intruders. They are the Romeros' security system. Rick notices right away that they're treated well enough, but—unlike some American pets—they're considered just animals, not cute honorary humans. Now and then Francisco tosses sticks for them to fetch or dangles a knotted rope for them to tug on, but otherwise he pays them little attention. Julio is even more matter-of-fact, basically ignoring them. Emiliana, who feeds them every day, will talk to them, but it's always in a mock-abusive tone. "So what do *you* want? You! And you! Good-for-nothing! Stop staring at me! You think I'll feed you just for wagging your tail?" The dogs eat only kitchen scraps: bits of half-spoiled meat, dried-out cheese, stale bread, and tortillas. No one pampers them, and Rick is sure that if Tizón and Sombra didn't pull their weight, they'd be gone in a flash.

The Romeros have a third pet: a crow that lives in a pale green metal cage suspended from the tree in the courtyard. Pure black, shiny, and so large that it can't sit on the perch without hunching, the crow does nothing but watch what goes on around it. Rick is aware of the bird's gaze following him. It's bad enough that the crow stares at him, first with one eye, then with the other. But it's the noise the crow makes—not a caw so much as a cough—that really bothers him. It's like the sound of fingernails on a blackboard, only louder, harsher, and even more grating.

Doesn't it bother anyone else? he wonders. *Don't the Romeros notice?* The bird calls constantly, and he winces every time. No one but him seems to care.

A Ton of Bricks

A man arrives with a truckload of *tabiques*—bricks. Helped by a couple of teenagers, he unloads two thousand of them from the flatbed onto the corner of Calle Aparicio and Callejón Hidalgo.

Over the past few weeks, Rick has hauled sand, crushed rock, and cement. He decides that bricks will probably be easier to carry, since they can be stacked. He's certain that he and the Romeros can make quick work of this task.

It doesn't take long for him to see that he's mistaken. Sand is relatively soft, and a *costal* adapts to the shape of the back and shoulders. Even a bag of cement, though stiffer, will shift a little against muscle and bone. But bricks are something else altogether.

Bricks aren't just hard, they're angular. They have edges, corners, and rock-hard surfaces. To make matters worse, these Mexican *tabiques* are bigger than American bricks—almost as big as small loaves of bread. They're also uneven in shape. Some are long and flat, others short and blocky. Looking at the long red-orange stack, Rick starts to imagine the ordeal ahead of him. These bricks are going to be a total pain in the butt—and back and arms and shoulders.

"How are we going to do this?" he asks Julio.

Julio makes his standard response to such questions: a low whistle through clenched teeth. Then he says, "Well, I guess we'll do the usual. Work like mules."

Rick reaches over to the pile of *tabiques* and picks one up. It weighs at least five pounds. At once he imagines a Mexican middle school math problem: *If* tabiques *weigh five pounds apiece, and* Julio carries sixteen *tabiques* in every load, *then*— He can't stand to make the calculation.

Every trip Rick makes is more difficult than the last. He loses his footing more and more often and struggles simply to keep a grip on the stack of bricks sloped against his back. Within a few hours, his muscles are burning with fatigue.

"It's time to rest."

Rick looks up to find Francisco crouched against a wall. He has dropped his load; *tabiques* lie scattered randomly around him.

"I'll be back in a minute," Rick tells him, anxious to make it all the way to the house with what he's carrying. But as soon as he speaks, the bricks become unbalanced and clatter to the ground. "Damn!" he shouts.

Francisco smiles. He pats the fallen bricks next to him. "Here," he says, "pull up a *tabique* and make yourself comfortable."

Rick is too tired to resist. He eases to the ground, arranges three bricks into a stack, then sits on them. "How many have we moved so far?" he asks.

Shrugging, Francisco says, "Maybe half."

Rick hears something to his left. Turning, he spots Julio approaching, his body hunched beneath a load of twenty or twenty-five bricks. *How can he carry so many bricks at once? He's the smallest guy among us!*

When Julio passes, he glances toward the boys for just a moment, unwilling to risk a misstep by taking his gaze from the path ahead.

"We'll get back to work soon," Francisco tells his father.

"Rest awhile, boys," he says, out of breath.

Rick doesn't feel right about sitting while Julio keeps slogging. "Is this okay?" he asks Francisco. "What we're doing?"

"Fine. He means it. Take it easy."

The boys stay seated. Rick can't believe how much his back hurts.

"What will you do once you've finished high school?" Francisco asks abruptly.

"Well, I'll definitely go to college," Rick says. "But I'm not sure which one . . ." He hesitates. He doesn't know the Spanish equivalent of "is right for me," so he gambles on the phrase *es lo mejor*, "is the best." Then, concerned that these words sound boastful, he adds, "Best for my interests, anyway."

Francisco blinks when he hears *lo mejor*. He asks, "So, then— which college will you actually attend?"

"Oh, I don't know," Rick replies. "I'm a pretty good student. The top schools wouldn't take me—you know, Harvard, Yale, Princeton, schools like that—but lots of others would." He flinches at the sound of his boastful words. Exhaustion seems to be making his tongue flap.

Francisco looks even more serious than usual; his expression is tight and withdrawn. Rick is worried that he's offended his friend, but Francisco continues the conversation. "What do you think you'll study?" he asks.

"I'm not sure," Rick replies. "I like writing and literature, so I'll pick a school that's strong in those subjects. I also like art history, and I'm interested in Latin American studies—that's another possibility. But I'm not sure if there's a school that's strong in *all* those areas . . ."

Belatedly, Rick realizes that he's babbling and that Francisco hasn't made eye contact with him for a while. In fact, Francisco is staring at the wall across the *callejón.* "What about you?" Rick asks abruptly, trying to shift the attention away from himself. "What'll you do after you finish school?"

"Teach," Francisco replies.

"Teaching is a good profession," Rick says. He pauses, but Francisco makes no other comment, so he blunders on. "Is that what you're interested in?"

Francisco looks perplexed. "Interested?"

"Are you interested in teaching?"

"It's a job. There's a local teachers' college that I've applied to. If I get accepted, I'll take the courses. Then maybe I can get a job. It pays pretty well—better than laying bricks does, anyway."

"That's great!" Rick says, aware that he sounds a bit too cheery. "Interesting work, too."

"First I have to get into the program," says Francisco. He stands up and starts stacking the bricks he'd dropped.

Rick realizes that by chattering on about his many educational options, he has annoyed or embarrassed Francisco. But he doesn't know what to say to smooth over the situation, so he, too, sets to work picking up the fallen *tabiques*.

They carry bricks all afternoon. They carry bricks until Rick stops thinking of himself as anything but a machine for moving bricks from one place to another. They carry bricks until around six that evening, when they move the last few *tabiques* from the far corner of the *callejón* to the Romeros' courtyard. Then, too tired even to eat supper, he eases himself up the stairs into the living room, collapses onto the sofa, and, still wearing his brick-dusty jeans and T-shirt, instantly falls asleep.

Time Travel

Church bells wake him. He lies in bed for a while, letting the complex tolling echo within his still-dormant brain.

It occurs to him that several kinds of bells are ringing. Some make a shallow racket—like brass pans clashing. Some are gongs that bong strongly, sound and silence lapsing into each other. Some toll . . . slow . . . dull.

Francisco lies on his mattress, across the room, still fast asleep. Impulsively, Rick gets out of bed, puts on clean clothes, and lets himself out into the alley. The morning is cool. It's just after dawn. No one else is up yet.

Climbing the hillside above the Romeros' house, he works his way among the cacti and mesquite trees, then turns abruptly. Santo Domingo lies spread out before him. A few lights sparkle through a blue-gray mist. A flock of birds flies across the gulf between the reddish-brown steeples of one church and the blue and white tiled dome of another. In the distance, where the town's outer edges diminish into little ranching communities, sunlight begins to spread over the land.

Rick watches for a while. Gazing out over the town—with its ancient towers, flat-roofed colonial houses, and cobblestone streets—he finds it hard to imagine that there are computers down there, or cell phones, fax machines, microwave ovens, and other modern gadgets. Santo Domingo looks lost in time, as if it's not the twenty-first century but the seventeenth. It's easy to see the place as it once was: a Mexican colonial town founded decades before the United States became a country.

What the hell am I doing here? he asks himself suddenly. Santo Domingo is fascinating but overwhelming. The Romeros have welcomed him, but he feels completely worn down by the demands of *la obra*. He's exhausted. His arms and legs ache. His back is so sensitive to touch that even the shirt he's wearing hurts his skin. It's hard to imagine doing anything but crawling right back into bed. Yet he knows that Julio has planned a whole series of construction tasks for the day.

How long can he keep going? How long can he deal with the stress of living this kind of life? Somehow the Romeros cope with it—but Rick isn't so sure that *he* can. Maybe he screwed up by coming here. Maybe his good intentions and enthusiasm aren't enough. Maybe he'll just embarrass himself and disappoint the Romeros. He has no clue what to do other than what he's already doing.

At last, too hungry to stand there and worry about the situation any longer, he starts wondering what Emiliana will fix for breakfast, then walks back to the house.

Toys

The children in the Romeros' neighborhood have few store-bought toys. At least Rick hasn't seen many. He's spotted some boys kicking around a soccer ball at the far end of Callejón Hidalgo and some others playing with marbles on a concrete slab jutting into the alley. Two days back he saw a little girl with a plastic doll. Other than that, the kids' toys are homemade—little paper boats to float in puddles, swords made of sticks, slingshots whittled out of forked tree branches, dolls made from rags and bits of string.

It's resourceful, he thinks; they have no money to buy stuff, so they improvise. And yet, scrambling up Callejón Catarata one afternoon, to where the steep street intersects with Callejón Hidalgo, he finds Hilaria and five other children flying tiny model airplanes.

He does a double take. *How is it possible?* he wonders. *How did they get such high-tech miniature toys?* Each airplane is just an inch long and buzzes this way and that on a delicate tether.

"*¿Qué hacen, chiquitos?*" he asks, baffled. What are you doing, kids?

"*Volando mayates,*" Hilaria explains. Flying *mayates.*

"What are *mayates*?" Rick asks.

The whole group stares in disbelief at such ignorance.

"Well, they're—*mayates,*" says Hilaria.

Her plane veers toward him on its tether, flying close enough for him to see it clearly. When he understands what he's seeing, he's amazed. It's not an airplane at all. It's a beetle—metallic green, iridescent, roughly the size of an American quarter. Somehow each kid has caught one of these insects, fastened a thread around its thorax, and coaxed it back into the air. Resourceful—and brilliant. Each *mayate* now buzzes around a kid, a live beetle orbiting its child-planet.

Bricklaying

"Today I'll teach you how to lay bricks," Julio announces.

Rick is pleased by this news. For all that he and the Romeros have accomplished so far, bricklaying seems a major step in their work on *la obra.*

After mixing a batch of *mezcla,* or mortar—a messy job that involves using shovels to combine sand, powdery white quicklime, and water—they set to work. Julio has already prepared an area right next to the living room. Two tall wooden stakes, set about eight feet apart, rise from where he has pounded them into the dirt. A string running along the ground connects one stake to the other. A second string, parallel to the first, connects the stakes about one yard off the ground. Together, the stakes and strings create a rectangle the size and shape of the wall that Rick and Julio will now create. This is the first wall of a room they'll build next to the living room, which is in the far corner of the property. Eventually, they'll build three other walls, including one right up against the living room itself.

It seems pretty straightforward to Rick, and he feels no anxiety about the task ahead. If anything, it'll be a relief after all the donkey work they've been doing.

Julio drags a shallow wooden box over to the staked-out area, then carries a load of *mezcla* and dumps it into the box. The thick stuff makes a slurpy, sloppy sound as it falls. Copying him, Rick brings a second load and dumps it.

"*Basta,*" Julio tells him. That's enough. Grasping a wooden-handled trowel that looks to Rick like a large cake server, Julio picks up his first scoop of *mezcla*. "I'll do a row," he says. "Then you can try it."

He lays down a neat puddle of *mezcla*. It's as grainy and gray as oatmeal. Somehow it goes down right against the string that runs along the ground, but no further. When Julio picks up a *tabique* and forces it onto the mortar, some of the gray stuff squishes out sideways, but a quick motion with the trowel slices off the excess. Julio flicks the little blob back into the mortar box.

"*Así lo hacemos.*" That's how we do it.

Julio proceeds to lay enough *tabiques* to form a line from one of the marking stakes to the other. He slaps some mortar between the bricks, which lie about half an inch apart, then neatly trims what oozes out sideways. The result looks tidy and strong.

Julio hands Rick the trowel. "Your turn," he says, his gold-framed front tooth flashing when he smiles.

Rick smiles back, but he feels hesitant. *This is the real thing,* he tells himself. Now he's not just *preparing* to build a house; he's actually building it. This wall has to carry its own weight. More than that! It has to carry the weight of the ceiling they'll eventually build on top of it and, later, the weight of a second floor and roof. He takes a deep breath, scoops some mortar from the box, and slops it onto the first row of bricks.

"*Ahí mero,*" says Julio. Right there.

It goes on fairly well—not as evenly as when Julio did it, but well enough. "*¿Más?*" he inquires. More?

"*Tantito.*" A little bit.

Rick adds to the gray blob. "*¿Está bien?*"

"*Perfecto.*"

Julio hands Rick two *tabiques.* One is full-sized; the other is half the normal length. Placing the half brick first allows the next to overlap properly with what's below, so that successive bricks don't line up too closely. Rick settles them into place. He scrapes the excess mortar off the sides just as Julio had done, then flicks what he gathers into the mortar box.

"What do you think?" he asks nervously.

"You're doing fine. Keep going." Julio looks pleased. His words, tone of voice, and expression all sound upbeat.

More confident now, Rick scoops more *mezcla* from the box, dumps it onto the first row of bricks, and sets another *tabique* into place. He repeats the process. Within a short period of time, he has laid the whole second row of bricks.

Julio whistles through his teeth. "*Híjole,* what can I say? You're so good, I should go hang up my trowel and let *you* build the house."

"Really?"

"I'm not kidding. You're a natural."

Rick is thrilled. For months he has worried about this phase of the project; now, suddenly, he's home free. He's surprised, however, when Julio pushes himself up, stands, and stretches. "Where are you going?" he asks.

"Somewhere else," Julio answers. "You sure don't need me *here.*"

"You want me to work on my own?"

"*¡Ándele!*" Go ahead.

Julio wanders off, lingers pensively in the courtyard for a moment, then starts to stack the used lumber that's lying in a heap nearby.

Rick resumes work. He trims the excess mortar off the second tier of bricks, then starts on the third. First a dab of mortar. Then a brick. Then a little trimming. It's all so easy that, watching his own hands at work, he laughs out loud in delight. The project will be a snap. With a seasoned pro like Julio and a gifted amateur like Rick, they'll have this whole house thrown together in a jiffy.

Mortar. Bricks. Mortar. Bricks. Mortar . . .

At one point, he stops to rest his arms—the effort is more

tiring than he'd expected—and notices with alarm that a long stretch of his wall is out of line. Each tier of bricks lies slightly closer to him than the one below, creating a bulge. He also notices that the wall isn't level; the right end of the top tier is a full inch higher than the left end. *How is it possible that I've already messed up?* he wonders. *I thought I was doing just great!*

Suddenly he hears Emiliana's crow. Tilting forward in its cage, it looks straight at him and caws raucously, as if it's mocking him.

He glances around. Julio is still stacking wood. Should he try fixing the wall himself? Maybe it's no big deal, and he should just let it go. Then, imagining it in ruins—collapsing in an earthquake, perhaps, or simply falling out of its own weakness—he calls out, "Don Julio?"

"*Sí.*"

"I've made a mistake."

Julio walks over. He sizes up Rick's work, viewing the wall from various angles, sighting down the tiers of bricks from the vantage of the string above. "It's all a matter of practice," he says, his features soft with patience. "You'll get the hang of it."

"What should I do?"

"Well, we'll have to take it apart and start over."

Rick feels terrible. "I'm really sorry!" he exclaims.

"Don't be," Julio says. He puts an arm around Rick's shoulder and gives him a fatherly hug. "You can't learn this work except by doing it. You're really good, believe me. It just takes a while to get it right."

Checking In

"It's been great," Rick says to his parents during the week's phone call. "The other day I built a brick wall for the first time."

"That's terrific," Dad says.

"I'm sure you did just fine," Mom says.

Annoyance passes over Rick like a wave of nausea. There's a condescending tone to her words. It's as if she assumes the past days' work is difficult, without first letting him describe it. As if she takes it for granted that he needs reassurance. "Yeah," he says at last, "I did just fine."

"Julio must be pleased."

"Yeah, the project is going well."

"And you're okay, too?" Mom asks.

"Of course."

"Eating well?"

"Emiliana is a terrific cook."

"And how are the Romeros, meanwhile?" Dad asks.

Rick glances at his watch. The call has already dragged on longer than he wanted. Several other customers are waiting to use the long-distance booth at Teléfonos de México. "They're fine. Look, I'd better go. We eat a big dinner at midday, and I don't want to be late."

"We won't keep you."

"Catch you next week."

"Give them our love."

Postcards

In the mail, Rick receives three postcards from friends back in Colorado. One is from Jason, his longtime pal and mountaineering partner. "Climbed Grays and Torreys peaks yesterday just to warm up for the season," Jason writes. "Went well—except for the threat of lightning on the way down. No bolts, though. Plan bigger expeditions for coming weeks."

The second postcard is from another friend, Al, who's working as a lifeguard at a private pool every day and taking a college-level astronomy course every evening. The picture on the card shows a bikini-clad woman. On the flip side, Al has written, "The mix of activities this summer seemed weird till I figured out what they had in common: close observation of heavenly bodies!"

The third postcard holds a scribbled note from Rick's former girlfriend. "Very boring here. Playing music, waitressing, trying to avoid the parents. Miss you. Sally."

Reading these messages, Rick feels oddly removed. It's as if hiking in the Rockies, watching swimmers in a pool, and working in a diner are exotic activities compared to what he's doing. He misses his buddies, though, especially Sally, who's a good friend despite their breakup. It's hard to believe that he won't see them again till late August.

A temptation hits him. He'll give them a call. Or he'll find Internet service somewhere in town and try to e-mail them. But at once he drops the idea; it'll make him homesick. Better to send postcards back, telling his friends what *he's* doing.

He buys a handful of cards—scenes of Santo Domingo—from a souvenir shop. But when he tries to write, he can only stare at the white space before him. How can he summarize what's happening? How can he explain *la obra,* his own part in it, or his growing closeness with the Romeros? He sits for a while with the cards untouched, then puts them away.

Work and Work and Work

Following each day's work, Emiliana serves a light supper, and Rick and the Romeros sit together in the kitchen till it's time for bed. Tonight she's made chicken soup with bits of carrot and squash, and she's toasted *bolillos*—tasty, thick-crusted rolls—on the griddle. The food is good, but Rick feels so drowsy in the dimly lit kitchen that he isn't sure he can stay awake until bedtime.

"We're doing fine," Julio announces. "We're making good progress."

"You two have been wonderful," Emiliana says. She smiles at both boys, but Rick notices that she looks at him a bit anxiously, perhaps mistaking his fatigue for boredom or discouragement.

He sits up straight. "What's next?" he asks quickly.

"We keep building the walls," Julio replies. "Then around Thursday this week we'll be ready to build *el castillo.*"

Rick is baffled. *Castillo* means castle. Clearly, Julio isn't planning to construct an entire castle, so something's being lost in translation. *"Castillo?"* he says. "I don't understand."

"Don't worry," says Julio. "I'll explain when we're ready."

"It's part of the cement work," says Francisco, getting ahead of his father.

Julio teases his son. "Don't confuse him. You'll spook the poor guy."

"I'm not spooking him."

"He'll think we're going to work him to death."

"No he won't." Francisco grins at Rick, hinting at a conspiracy between them. "He knows what's happening."

"He'll run away and go home."

They kid around for a while longer, and Rick just listens, comfortable with the good-natured teasing.

"More food?" Emiliana asks.

Rick shakes his head. "No thanks—I'm full."

They talk about what to do after supper. It's only eight o'clock. Rick feels ready for bed but doesn't want to snub the Romeros' hospitality. They own a TV but rarely use it because it has no antenna and gets poor reception. Hanging out makes more sense—chatting about what has happened that day, hearing about one another's activities, telling stories.

"¿Cómo está la vida allá en el norte?" asks Julio. The Romeros never refer to the United States by name; instead, they say "over there in the north," or simply "in the north."

Rick isn't sure what Julio is asking. Does he mean how's life with your family, or how's life in America more generally? "We're fine," he says, just to be safe. "Things are fine."

"You like it there?" Francisco asks.

Now Rick realizes that their curiosity is more general. "Sure, I like it," he replies guardedly. How can he explain? He feels lucky to be an American, to have a life without hardship, to have so many options available to him. At the same time, he's uneasy about many aspects of American culture and about issues facing the country—poverty . . . materialism . . . crime . . . pollution . . . racial tensions. To complicate matters, he isn't sure that he can discuss these things in Spanish. At last he says, "Life is good there but very . . . rushed."

"Rushed," echoes Emiliana.

Rick has used the phrase *hecho a toda prisa*, meaning "done with great haste," but he isn't sure it's the best choice. "Everyone is always racing around, doing eight things at once," he explains. "People are worried about the future."

Emiliana nods, but she looks perplexed. "What are they worried about?"

"Well, we have our share of problems."

"There's plenty of work, though," says Julio firmly, as if that settled the matter.

"There's work for most people. But still . . . " Rick falters, then goes on. As he tries to describe political and social concerns, he's more and more aware of the Romeros' bafflement. He realizes that nothing he says will convince them that life in the United States is frustrating or challenging for a middle-class kid like him. Or perhaps for anyone. "It's hard to explain," he ends lamely. Then, eager to change the subject, he asks, "What about you? Tell me something about your lives."

Julio and Emiliana glance at one another, smiling. "There's not much to say," Julio tells him.

"We're just ordinary people," adds Emiliana with a shrug.

"Not at all," Rick assures them. "And you're my friends, so I'm curious."

The Romeros exchange more glances. They seem surprised by Rick's interest.

"*Tell* him something," Francisco says, as if annoyed about his parents' reticence.

Julio shrugs. "Well?" he asks, nodding to his wife.

"No," says Emiliana. "*You* first."

So Julio proceeds. He speaks plainly, in the lilting accent of central Mexico. Born forty-six years ago in a little farming community called Los Jacales—the Shacks—he grew up in poverty, the youngest of six brothers and two sisters. "*Pues, ¡comíamos puros nopales!*" he exclaims at one point. We ate nothing but cactus leaves!—a statement that Rick realizes is an exaggeration, though he knows that some Mexicans do, in fact, eat fried *nopales*.

"My father didn't like kids very much," Julio continues. "He hit us a lot and dressed us in rags. My brothers left home as soon as possible. Then I had to tend the fields alone—plowing, sowing, harvesting. We lived on borrowed land and didn't earn much, so I never got paid—*ni un centavo*." Not even a penny.

Emiliana nods as her husband speaks. Francisco listens quietly.

Julio slices a *bolillo* in half, spreads one part with margarine, and tops it with strawberry jam.

"Once my father whipped me till I passed out. I woke up when it was dark and walked to Santo Domingo, which took me all night. I hid in a rocky place above town so he wouldn't find me. Then a man with some dogs came. He owned the land and had seen me, so he came to check me out. I explained that my father was cruel and I'd run away. The man understood. He took me to his home to sort beans. He paid me fifty *centavos* a day."

Julio pauses to take a bite of his *bolillo,* then goes on. "For three days I sorted beans and hoped my father wouldn't find me, but he did. He tried to act friendly. He said, 'You don't want to work here. Come home where you've at least got something to eat.' Well, back home we had corn, but my father always sold it to buy tequila. I refused to go with him, even after he threatened me. And guess who else left him? My mother! My father had beaten her after I'd run away, so she cleared out while he was in Santo Domingo. My sisters left soon after that. Then Father was all alone at Los Jacales.

"I stayed here in town. First I worked as a baker. Then I learned masonry and construction. I've also traveled to Texas three times to earn some extra money."

When it's clear that Julio has finished speaking, Rick doesn't know what to say. Words like "What a hard life!" would sound stupid and cheap. And apologies—"I'm sorry it's been so difficult"— would seem odd, since nothing about Julio's story suggests that he expects or wants pity. He's simply stated the facts and then fallen silent. He appears more intent on finishing his supper than on hearing anyone's response.

Rick finds this lull awkward at first, then intolerable. "How about you, doña Emiliana?" he finally asks, breaking the stillness.

"Me?" she replies, pursing her lips in a faint smile.

"I'd love to hear about your life, too."

"What's to say about an old woman?"

Rick knows that she's being coy. "Tell me just a little," he says.

She begins as Julio did, calmly, almost without emotion. She explains that she grew up in central Mexico, in the city of Guanajuato, a center for silver mining. Despite the town's wealth, her family was poor, and she worked as a servant from the time she was eight or nine years old. In her teens, she took a job with one of the richest families in Guanajuato. The pay was reliable but low; the conditions were tough. She worked twelve to sixteen hours a day, six days a week. Her employers prohibited the servants from leaving the house except to go to Mass on Sunday mornings. When they discovered that some of the girls were meeting their boyfriends in church, they took away that Sunday privilege. Emiliana was so outraged that she quit and moved to Santo Domingo.

"After a couple of jobs with Mexican families," she says, "I went to work for an *americano* at a somewhat better salary. I didn't really care who I worked for so long as they paid me and treated me well. Sometimes they did; sometimes they didn't. I mean both the Mexicans and the *americanos*. The truth is, the people who can afford a servant aren't necessarily the kind of folks who treat you well.

"But there was another issue. Mexican families resented the *americanos* for hiring servants and paying them better. The Mexicans felt that made them look bad. Before long, they went to a priest for support. He was sympathetic and called a number of us together. 'Don't you understand what you're dealing with?' he asked. 'Many of these people aren't Catholics. Some are even atheists.' He said that if we persisted in working for *americanos,* he'd threaten us with excommunication.

"Well, I didn't like that one bit. I'm a good Catholic—God knows that—but I stood up to him. 'I have a right to better my life,' I said. 'It doesn't matter to me if my employer is an atheist, just as long as he treats me right and pays me properly. If you want to excommunicate me, go ahead. The real discussion will occur when I die and face God myself.'"

Emiliana pauses, taking a sip from her tea. She looks so grandmotherly, so prim—with her little finger extended as she holds her cup—that Rick finds it hard to imagine her talking back to a priest.

Julio grins broadly, his gold tooth flashing. "Don't ever get my wife angry!" he exclaims. "She's big trouble."

They all chuckle, even Emiliana. Then she continues.

"After I married don Julio, I kept working as a servant. We wanted to buy some property, a house. This dream stayed a dream for many years, because saving money was almost impossible. But we kept going. Don Julio worked; I worked; and once Francisco came along and reached nine or ten years old, he worked, too."

As Emiliana speaks, her voice grows higher, louder, and more animated. She sits straight-backed and rarely gestures, but her facial expressions reveal the same frustration that her voice does. "There are those of us who are poor, who work and work and work and never realize that things should be better," she says. "Then there are those of us who *know* that things should be better, and we, too, just work and work and work."

She falls silent.

Rick feels intensely uncomfortable. If he was uncertain about what to say after Julio's story, he's completely tongue-tied after Emiliana's.

She seems to pick up on his discomfort, for she suddenly waves her right hand back and forth as if to disperse the dark mood she has cast over the gathering. "Enough!" she exclaims. "Enough sad stories!" Then, turning to her son, with a sweet smile, she asks, "And you? What do *you* have to say?"

Francisco huffs in amusement. "Me? I say we're boring our guest."

"Not at all," Rick protests. "I've enjoyed this."

"Forgive us," says Emiliana, resting a hand on his forearm.

"Please don't apologize."

"We're all tired," says Julio, standing. "We could talk all night, but we shouldn't. We have lots of work ahead of us tomorrow."

Insomnia

The local dogs keep Rick awake that night—not just the neighbors' dogs, but Tizón and Sombra, too, in an endless litany of yapping, of howl and counter-howl.

Woo! Woo-WOO! Woo-woo-woo-woo-WOO!

Rick ignores them at first, then tries to block their noise by sticking bits of cotton in his ears. But it's not just the dogs that are bothering him. His mind is yapping at him, as well. He can't shake the evening's conversation. If Julio and Emiliana had been more dramatic—telling woeful tales, bemoaning their hardships, screaming about the heartless rich—he'd feel less haunted. Instead, they were the opposite, so . . . so undramatic, nondramatic, whatever the word might be. Julio, especially.

Rick dozes off, then jolts awake when yet another chorus begins.

Woo-woo-woo-woo-woo-woo-WOO!

What was he thinking about? Oh, yeah—Julio's story. It had surprised him because it was told without anger. Julio seemed resigned, almost amused, by what he'd gone through. It was as if difficulties washed over him like rain, and he just dried himself off and kept going.

Emiliana's story was different. She spoke in a straightforward way, but there was a quiet fury beneath her words. It was clear that she felt the sting of the misdeeds done to her. She was angry that the injustices hadn't been corrected, and she didn't mind expressing her anger.

Rick realizes that if there's ever a revolution in Mexico, she'll be marching with the rebels while Julio watches from a safe distance.

And Francisco? What does he feel? He was silent during his parents' narrations. He offered no comments, no sympathy. Was he unconcerned by what they said—or, more likely, just bored? Maybe he'd heard it all before. Maybe hearing about Julio's and Emiliana's hardships made him feel the way Rick has felt when listening to stories about *his* parents' past difficulties.

What should I do? he wonders. *What do the Romeros expect from me?* Mulling things over, he dozes off again.

Woo-woo-WOO!

Jolted awake, he throws off the covers and looks around. Francisco is fast asleep and snoring softly. How does the guy manage it, with such a racket going on?

Once again Rick feels overwhelmed, but he isn't sure why.

He isn't even sure what's bothering him. Is it Julio and Emiliana? Is it Francisco? Is it what they expect of him? It's all of these things and none of them.

Woo-woo-woo-woo-WOO!

Rick stomps over to the window, pulls it open, and—loud as he can—shouts, "SHUT UP!" His outburst sets off another round of barking. He's furious now, actually shaking with rage. But suddenly he realizes that he has shouted in English instead of Spanish. He leans out again and screams, *"¡CÁLLENSE!"* which, predictably, turns up the canine volume even higher.

Crossing Paths

One day when Julio gives the boys the afternoon off, Rick walks to town and wanders alone through the *jardín público*. He has his camera along and snaps some pictures, but mostly he just enjoys watching all the people. Four Mexican toddlers chase pigeons on the sidewalk. Two elderly American couples on adjacent park benches discuss their visits to other scenic towns. Vendors patrol the perimeter like sentries, accosting tourists as they enter the *jardín*. An American woman lets her leashed golden retriever puppy lick an ice cream cone while two beggar kids watch solemnly from a few feet away.

Another interaction catches his eye. A teenaged gringa is negotiating with a vendor of blankets and handwoven textiles. The vendor, a middle-aged Mexican man, is smiling, but he and the girl seem to have reached an impasse, and they both look frustrated. *Small wonder,* Rick thinks, when he overhears some of their conversation. The gringa is speaking English to the vendor, even though he signals that he doesn't understand her language.

Rick is ready to ignore them when the gringa turns slightly. At once Rick realizes that she's the redhead he saw a few weeks earlier—the one who smiled at him—so he walks over and says, "Excuse me . . . Need some help?"

She turns toward him and gives him a puzzled smile.

"I mean, you know, translating," Rick adds quickly. He's on the verge of getting tongue-tied. The girl is even prettier than he first thought, with gray-green eyes and freckles scattered across high cheekbones.

"Well—that'd be nice," she says.

"*Yo puedo traducir,*" Rick tells the vendor. I can translate.

"*Espero que sí,*" the vendor replies, meaning both "I hope you can" and "I'll bet you can."

The girl gestures in frustration. "He seems to think I'm trying to lower the price too far, but I'm not. I don't have a problem with his price. The problem is, I don't have enough money with me, so I have to go home"—she waves toward the distant hills—"to get more. But I'd like him to hold the shawl for me."

Rick explains to the vendor, who nods, now grasping the situation.

"Tell him I'll be back around five today."

He relays this message; the crisis ends. The vendor leaves content (winking at Rick), and Rick finds himself alone with the girl.

"Thanks for helping me," she says. "I'm afraid I don't speak much Spanish."

"No problem."

"That was so embarrassing."

"It seemed like a simple misunderstanding."

"Maybe—but you probably think I'm an idiot."

"Not at all."

They stand there awkwardly for a long moment just looking at each other. Rick is so pleased to be standing next to her that he feels almost dizzy.

"My name's Ellen," she says.

"I'm Rick Dresner."

"I think I saw you here once before. Are you American?"

He nods. "You, too?"

"Yes. From California—the Bay Area." Then she adds, "You speak Spanish pretty well."

"I'm working on it."

Without discussing what to do, they start walking together through the *jardín*. The town clock strikes three. It's hot now. Few Mexicans stay out in the midday sun, so most of the people lingering in the park are gringos. Rick and Ellen wind their way among the tourists clustered on the tiled sidewalks.

"I love this place," says Ellen. She makes a swirling gesture with one hand, as if to gather in all of Santo Domingo. "Not just because it's so beautiful . . . but because it's so calm and friendly, too. I feel like I'm living in another century."

"Ever been to this part of Mexico before?"

"No—first time."

"Just passing through?" Rick asks, thinking it would be great if Ellen were staying in town awhile.

"I'm visiting my dad. My sisters and I spend part of each summer with him, and he just bought a house here."

"He's Mexican?" Rick inquires idly.

"No, he just likes the area. Most of the time, he lives in Palo Alto. My mom lives in Marin County. They're divorced." She glances his way. "How about you?"

"I'm from Denver. I'm visiting friends—staying with them all summer." He gestures toward the high end of Santo Domingo. "Up the hill."

Ellen smiles. "Really? We live up there, too. We must be neighbors."

"Cool." Immediately he starts to imagine exploring the town with her. They could find a nice place to hang out . . .

Before he can speak, though, Ellen says, "You know, I'd better go home and get some money so I can keep my promise to that weaver guy."

"It's just three o'clock."

"I know, but I'd still better go."

Rick feels disappointed; maybe she's trying to shake him. Then he gets an idea. "I'm heading that way, too. How about if we walk together?"

She looks amused. "It's way up there. I'll just take a cab."

He decides not to press the issue. Ellen clearly wants to be alone, and he doesn't want to annoy her by insisting. But he can't help wonder where, exactly, "way up there" is. There are many houses overlooking Santo Domingo. How far away is her father's?

"Some other time," he suggests.

"Sure."

They walk to one of the corners of the *jardín* and take the stair-case to the street. There's a taxi stand with several cabs waiting.

Rick decides to try one last time. "Maybe I could give you a call . . . "

Ellen ignores him. She says, *"Buenas tardes,"* to the cab driver, who looks so delighted to have this pretty gringa as a passenger that he opens the door for her ceremoniously. She climbs in.

"Thanks again for your help, Rick," she says through the open window.

"Anytime," he replies, feeling stung.

She turns aside, looking at her lap. Then, as the driver prepares to pull away, she reaches out with a slip of paper she's apparently been scribbling on. "Here's my number," she says.

Rick takes the paper. He can barely hide his delight.

Mother's Helper

Hilaria shows up at the Romeros' house two or three times a week. Staying there all day, she helps Emiliana with a nearly un-ending series of chores. She washes the breakfast dishes in a metal tub that sits beneath the property's only water faucet. She wipes the kitchen table and sweeps the floor. She runs market errands with Emiliana, returning with plastic mesh bags that bulge with vegetables, fruits, beans, meat, bread, and tortillas. She helps sweep the floors and do the laundry. She works and works and works.

Rick watches in astonishment whenever his own activities

allow. Hilaria does all these chores without whining or bellyaching. An American kid her age wouldn't last an hour doing what she does, much less a whole day. What makes it possible for her to stand all the work?

It's obvious that the girl adores her aunt, and Emiliana certainly treats her with great affection and respect. There's never an impatient word or scolding. Hovering like a plump hen with a tiny chick, Emiliana teaches Hilaria cooking, cleaning, and other domestic skills that she seems not to have learned from her own mother. Hilaria watches her aunt with a constant smile, and Emiliana observes her niece with obvious pride and affection. The warmth between them is so intense that Rick can almost bask in its glow.

"¿Qué hago ahora, Tía?" asks Hilaria in her high, singsong voice. What shall I do now, Auntie?

"Well—rest a moment."

"No, no, Auntie. I want to do something more."

When Emiliana at last convinces Hilaria to take a break, Rick detects another reason for the girl's presence in the house: curiosity about him. She comes and stands a few feet away from the wall he's building, staring at him with an intensity that he's seen only in much younger children.

"¿Qué tal, pues?" he asks her. Well, how's it going?

"Muy bien, gringuito."

"Are you feeling well?"

"Very well."

"How's your family?"

"My mother is sick," she states blandly. "My father is drunk."

"I see."

"He's always drunk."

"Oh," says Rick, slightly embarrassed by the girl's blunt comments.

"My mother says he's the most worthless man in town."

"Is that so?"

"She says he's the most worthless man in the whole state."

"Really."

"She says—"

"What do you think of my wall?" Rick asks, trying to change the subject.

Hilaria squats to get a better look. *"Muy mal. Está chueca,"* she states. Very bad. It's crooked.

"I'll fix it," Rick says quickly.

"You'd better. Even my dad lays bricks better than you!"

He's embarrassed—humiliated, really—by this comparison. "I said I'd fix it."

"Even when he's drunk!"

Rick starts pulling bricks off the still-wet mortar.

Hilaria asks, "Are you drunk, *gringuito*?"

"Of course not."

At that moment, Rick hears Emiliana calling out from the kitchen: *"Hilaria, déjalo en paz."* Leave him in peace.

Hilaria smiles abruptly, showing her tiny, perfect teeth.

Emiliana calls once again: *"¡Hilaria! ¡Vente!"* Come here!

"I'll be right there, Auntie!"

It's mealtime that reveals the most basic reason for the girl's presence. Assisting her aunt, Hilaria serves the menfolk—Rick first, since he's the guest; then Julio, since he's the oldest male; then Francisco. The

meal starts with soup, proceeds to turkey in a sauce made of pump-
kin seeds and spices, then moves on to stuffed chiles, rice, and sautéed squash. The men have been eating for five minutes by the time
Emiliana gets around to serving herself and Hilaria.

Rick has been uncomfortable with this men-first setup from
the early days of his visit, but he's never felt right about meddling
with the Romeros' customs. His solution has been to eat slowly,
which allows Emiliana and Hilaria to catch up. This also lets him
watch what the little girl is doing.

Hilaria looks almost dizzy as she stares at the feast. Uncon-
scious of her actions, she starts bouncing on her toes. "Meat!" she
exclaims. "Meat, meat, meat! And soup!"

"Calm down," Emiliana tells her gently. "In a moment it'll be
your turn."

When at last Emiliana sets a plate before the girl, Hilaria devours her meal with such eagerness that she appears unaware of
the people around her. That's when Rick realizes why, whatever
else the payoff, she has worked so hard and so patiently.

Bells

The bells of Santo Domingo toll off and on all day long. Sometimes it's one bell, just a slow *bong . . . bong . . . bong . . .* noting the
hour. Sometimes two bells sound at once, quickly, almost frantically, as if competing to summon the faithful to Mass. And on

Sunday mornings, dozens of bells seem to let loose simultaneously, pealing so hard that the air throbs with noise. Rick can hold
his hand to the door, then, and feel it vibrate in response.

He isn't Catholic, so he doesn't feel that the church bells call
out to him with their ancient invitation. Even so, they affect him.
Their deep resonance changes his state of mind, calming him
when he's stressed and giving him energy when he's tired. It's not
something that he can explain. He can only feel it deep within
his bones.

The Crow

"What does the crow do, anyway?" Rick asks Emiliana one day
after listening to its annoying and endless coughlike caw.

"Do?" She seems surprised by the inquiry.

Perhaps he hasn't put the question right. What he meant was,
does it have some specific function, as Tizón and Sombra do? He
tries again to muster the Spanish words. *"¿Cómo se sirve?"*

Emiliana still seems puzzled. *"¿Sirve?"*

Rick isn't sure if he'd said what he intended. He'd meant to
say, "What purpose does it serve?" But maybe the words he'd
used *actually* meant, "How do you serve it?" An image floats into
his head: Emiliana presenting him with a platter covered by a silver dome. She whisks off the polished lid, and—voilà!—there's a
roasted crow on the plate.

He feels himself blush. *"No. ¿Cuál es el significado del cuervo?"* What's the significance of the crow?

Now Emiliana laughs outright.

Rick laughs, too. "Sorry. I'm not making sense."

"Don't worry, Ricardo—you're doing fine."

He can't believe it's so hard to carry on such a basic conversation. What did all those years of Spanish class do for him? Where are the words? Even when he finds them, he can't hook them together right. All the while, the crow coughs in contempt at his efforts.

"¡Qué animal tan extraño!" he exclaims. What a strange animal! Then at once he regrets this comment.

"Don't you like him?" Emiliana asks, her face abruptly serious.

"No, it's not that."

"Does he bother you?"

"Not at all." Rick struggles to backtrack. "What I meant—"

"Because if he does . . ."

"I like him, I like him!" Rick says. He gestures with both hands, opening his arms in something like a hug, hoping she won't detect the lie.

"Truly?" she asks.

"Truly. He's wonderful! Fascinating! Very unusual!"

Only on hearing these exclamations does Emiliana's concern seem to ease.

El Barrio

When Rick first arrived in Santo Domingo, he figured that the barrio would be a neighborly kind of place. Poverty would unite people, and they'd look after one another. This hasn't turned out to be true. People live in close quarters—small homes wedged together all over the hillside—but they don't interact much. Yes, neighbors greet one another in passing. Yes, they sometimes hang out and talk in the street (usually men with men, women with women). But otherwise they spend most of their time with their own families. Far from uniting people, poverty seems to keep them apart. Why, Rick can't tell. Maybe it's because their own troubles are enough of a burden.

Even the Romeros' ties with their own relatives are looser than he'd expected. Mexico is the land of the extended family. It's one for all and all for one, or so he'd been told. The Romeros do, in fact, have a large number of relatives nearby—brothers and sisters, uncles and aunts, nephews and nieces. Emiliana's sister Carmen visits the Romeros regularly. Old Aniseto totters by every once in a while. Hilaria spends a lot of time with Emiliana, and Hilaria's ten-year-old sister, Remedios, stops by occasionally. But though the Romeros clearly cherish *some* of these family members, others aren't quite so welcome in their home. For example, they consider Juan's oldest son, Rodolfo, to be lazy and unreliable. And Juan himself receives their deepest scorn: he's a drunk and a dreamer whose irresponsibility causes his entire family great pain.

At some point it occurs to Rick that relationships here aren't much different from those in America. The barrio isn't a huge, seamless fabric any more than his own neighborhood is. There's something oddly reassuring about this insight, but it doesn't make him feel any less of an outsider.

Rick and Julio are in the courtyard one morning when two teenage boys show up.

"*Qué tal, Tío,*" says one of the boys as they descend the stairs.

Julio is clearly delighted. "*Pues, ¡mira quién llega!*" he exclaims. Hey, look who's here!

The boys turn out to be Alfonso and Lucho, Juan's second and third sons. Julio and his nephews shake hands with surprising formality, then stand around exchanging cheerful insults. Rick watches, feeling awkward, until Julio introduces him.

"Rick is visiting us from *el norte,*" states Julio.

Alfonso and Lucho nod simultaneously.

"He's helping us build our house."

Again they nod.

These two brothers would look almost alike—muscular and wide-shouldered, with curly hair and hazel eyes—except that some illness or accident has damaged Lucho's face. Large splotches of pink wrinkled skin cover his cheeks, neck, and forehead. Rick tries to force his attention elsewhere. *What happened?* he wonders. *A skin disease? Burns?*

Rick tries to chat with the brothers, but they are so shy, they barely respond to his comments and questions, and neither one looks him in the eye. Just a few minutes pass before they head back up the stairs.

"Nos vemos," announces Alfonso. See you later. And they're gone.

"Did I offend them?" Rick asks Julio once the door slams shut.

"Offend?" He looks puzzled.

"They were in such a hurry to leave."

"Not at all," Julio says. "They're just busy. They support their entire family, so they're always on the move—either working or looking for work."

Rick feels reassured. He's about to drop the subject of the boys, but then his curiosity gets the better of him and he asks, "What happened to Lucho? You know—to his face."

"Fuegos artificiales," replies Julio.

Rick doesn't understand. *Fuegos* means "fires," and *artificiales* is clearly "artificial." But "artificial fires"? He fetches his dictionary and looks up the words. *"Fuegos artificiales.* Fireworks," he reads.

Julio explains. "Lucho worked for a while in a fireworks factory. There was an accident—an explosion and a fire—and he was badly burned. We almost lost him."

"He's okay now?"

"Fine. Except, of course, for his appearance," Julio replies. "He's a good boy. So is Alfonso. I wish Juan were even half what they are."

He Got Away

When Rick gets up one morning, the first thing he notices is a change in what he hears. Something is missing. Now and then the dogs bark, and there's the usual background noise of radios blaring here and there in the barrio. But some sound that has long bothered him is absent. He just can't figure out what it is.

When he crosses the courtyard on his way to the kitchen, he realizes what's made the difference. The birdcage is empty.

Emiliana is standing at the burners, frying eggs. *"Buenos días,"* he says to her.

"Buenos días." She looks up and smiles. "Did you sleep well?"

"Very well, thanks." Rick sits down at the table behind her. After a moment's hesitance he asks, "What happened to the crow?"

"The crow?" Emiliana doesn't turn to face him.

"Your pet crow."

"Oh, him. He got away."

Rick is relieved. *Good riddance!* he thinks. The crow's cawing was so annoying. But then its escape starts to puzzle him. The latch on the cage looked tricky—not the sort of mechanism that a bird could have sprung by accident or even on purpose. Hilaria might have let it out, but neither she nor any other kid has visited for several days. Besides, the cage hangs too high on the *pirul* tree for her to reach without help. Only an adult could have released the crow.

"Would you like bread or tortillas with your eggs?" Emiliana asks him.

"Bread, please."

"Plain or toasted?"

"Toasted, please."

Emiliana doesn't seem angry or annoyed, Rick notes, but there's something odd about her behavior this morning. She has a mischievous air, as if she's withholding information. Something about the crow?

Abruptly, Rick realizes that Emiliana herself must have sprung the crow from its cage. He realizes, too, that she didn't do it for the bird's sake or because *she* wanted to be rid of it, but because Rick had commented on the crow's presence. What, exactly, had he said? He can't even remember. But it must have caught her attention and caused her to feel that the crow was a flaw in her hospitality. Rick didn't like her pet? The pet had to go.

No one says anything more about the bird, but as Rick eats his breakfast, he can't help wondering what *else* his hosts would change if he expressed dissatisfaction. Would they get rid of Tizón and Sombra if he complained about their barking? Would they switch rooms with him if he complained about sleeping on the couch? Would they cook different meals if he complained about the food? He tries to think of any other comments he's made—comments that his hosts may have taken to heart. What else might they do for him just because he's made a few offhand remarks? It's a little scary to contemplate.

Vocabulary

Julio, Francisco, and Rick have finished building the walls for the new room. It's an open box at this point—a box without a lid. Now they begin constructing *el castillo*—which turns out to be a framework of steel rods and wire that rises vertically at the walls' corners and horizontally along their upper edges. Once encased in concrete, this framework will help support the roof that they'll build to cap the room at a later stage of the project.

All goes well at first. Then Julio encounters a problem: he has trouble getting the *castillo* to fit right on the front wall of the new room. He explains that if it doesn't fit properly, it will cause problems later on, damaging or even ruining the structural integrity of the building. Standing on a ladder, leaning over the edge of the *castillo*, he struggles for an hour and then decides that this task can't be accomplished from inside the room. He climbs all the way up the ladder, eases onto the *castillo* itself, and crouches there on the narrow rim, facing the boys ten feet below.

"What are you doing?" Francisco asks his father.

"*Un momentito,*" is the only response. Just a moment.

Rick watches uneasily. When Julio beckons, he quickly climbs partway up the ladder. His chest is now at the same level as the *castillo*. He can watch Julio and even reach out to him if necessary. But he doesn't understand what Julio is doing there in the first place. He seems to be fiddling with the steel structure to his right, making adjustments to something with one hand while grasping the top of the wall with the other.

Still crouching on the metal framework, Julio eases himself sideways. Rick feels jittery to see him in such a precarious position. A slip will send Julio plummeting backwards into the *callejón* to break his back or crack his skull. Yet he proceeds without any visible alarm, his eyes looking amused and his mouth curved in a slight smile.

"*Tráeme el martillo,*" he tells Francisco, who leaves at once.

Rick knows that *tráeme* means "bring me," but he wonders what a *martillo* is.

"Dame la mano," Julio tells Rick. Give me your hand.

Rick reaches out across the *castillo,* and they clasp left hands.

"Agárrame fuerte."

Rick figures this out quickly; Julio is telling him to hold on tight. So he grips Julio's hand even harder than before.

Julio proceeds a short distance further along the rim of the *castillo.* Then, with his right hand, he starts tugging at something Rick can't see. Rick braces himself against the ladder and struggles to keep a good grip.

"Ahora sí estamos bien," Julio states, sounding pleased. Now we're fine.

He continues his efforts, and Rick starts to wonder how long he can keep holding on. He has begun to sweat, and his left palm feels so slippery that he has trouble clasping Julio's hand. "How's it going?" he asks, dismayed by the fear he hears in his voice.

"Fine, just fine."

"How long do you think this will take?"

"Oh, not much longer."

Rick feels relieved. His arm and shoulder have begun to tremble.

Somewhere below in the courtyard, Tizón and Sombra start to bark frantically.

Suddenly, Julio shouts, *"¡Suéltame! ¡Suéltame!"*

Rick hears the urgent tone but has no idea what the word means. Hold on? Help me? Or something else?

Julio shoots him a quick glance. He's fumbling with his right hand. *"¡Suéltame!"* he calls out again.

Rick holds on even tighter. He can't believe that Julio wants to be released—he seems on the verge of falling—so he assumes that he should hang on.

He hears footsteps at his back and glances over his shoulder to see Francisco approaching, a hammer in his hand. The boy looks horrified by whatever's going on. At that moment, Julio yanks his left hand out of Rick's slippery grip.

"No!" Rick shouts reflexively, convinced that Julio will topple backwards. But Julio remains safely on his perch. Then, to Rick's relief and delight, he starts to ease back across the top of the *castillo*.

Francisco steps closer and gives Rick the hammer he'd brought up from the patio. Rick passes it on to Julio.

"*Gracias,*" says Julio.

For several minutes, Julio does whatever he's doing: fastening, fixing. Rick waits, breathing hard. By now he is sweating from head to toe. He's ready to offer Julio more help, but he feels so shaken by whatever just went wrong that he's reluctant to speak. What was the problem, anyway? He can't figure it out. Then Julio scoots back to the ladder, and they both climb down into the empty room.

Sitting on the patio steps after the midday meal, Rick flips through his dictionary. There is no entry for *suéltame* and nothing for any of the likely infinitives—*sueltar, suelter,* or *sueltir.* He turns the pages, poking around to see if he's missed something. Then he realizes his mistake. He's looking for one of those tricky Spanish verbs that change their spelling when used as a command. The word he wants is *soltar.* He finds it at once.

"Soltar," he reads out loud. "To unfasten, loosen; to turn loose; to cast off; to set free, let go . . ."

Julio just wanted him to let go.

Rick sits for a while, wondering if Julio is angry with him. If he resents Rick for the confusion that took place on the wall. He'd said nothing about the incident; he'd simply smiled and thanked Rick before proceeding with his next task. There was no sign of emotion other than calm appreciation. But somehow this non-response makes Rick feel profoundly uneasy. How many other misunderstandings will the Romeros have to tolerate? What are the odds that he'll make such a big mistake that someone gets seriously hurt?

Rick imagines all sorts of awful scenarios, and despite the midday heat, he shivers.

Panic

For three whole days in mid-July, working from dawn almost straight through till dusk, Rick, Julio, and Francisco carry building materials. They carry another ton of lumpy crushed *grava,* bag after bag, up the steep *callejón.* Almost at once a new delivery arrives: sixty ten-foot lengths of *varilla*—thin steel rebar used to create reinforcing grids for concrete. They lug these rods to the house, too, and stack them neatly wherever they can find the storage space. Just as they finish hauling the *varilla,* yet another batch of cement demands their attention: thirty sacks weighing sixty-six pounds apiece.

By nightfall each day, Rick is so tired that he can barely stay awake through supper. A nine-thirty bedtime seems like an oasis in a vast desert, and collapsing onto the sofa means falling instantly asleep. Then, after what seems only the blink of an eye, he awakens to full daylight, birdsong, and throbbing muscles, and the tasks of *la obra* start all over again.

A swell of panic rises from deep within Rick. Will he ever adjust to these people, to their town, to their way of life? Will he manage to perform the tasks ahead? Will he be strong enough to do the work and have the stamina to keep going day after day? Can he keep learning new construction skills? The truth is that *la obra* scares him half to death. How are two seventeen-year-olds and a middle-aged man going to manage? By themselves. Without power tools. Even if he's physically capable of doing his share, will he understand what Julio asks of him, or will his shoddy Spanish get them all in trouble?

With his mind buzzing and his whole body aching, Rick wonders if he should do everyone a favor and just go home.

II

Muddling Through

Another delivery arrives at the corner of Callejón Hidalgo and Calle Aparicio. At first Rick figures that it's scrap lumber; all the boards are rough-edged and gray. Then he sees that the materials are more regularly shaped than he first thought. There's a pile of beams, maybe five or six dozen of them, each about eight feet long. There's also a stack of fifty or sixty wooden squares, each approximately two feet on a side. Combined, these two heaps of lumber would be as big as a truck.

"What's all this stuff?" Rick asks Julio and Francisco.

"*Vigas y cimbra,*" Francisco responds, pointing first to the beams, then to the squares. "They're used to support the new concrete ceiling while it dries."

"We'll build a framework of beams inside the new room," Julio explains. He raises three fingers of his left hand, holding them upright like pillars. Then he places his right index finger along the upright fingers to form a crosspiece. "If we nail the framework just right, it'll be quite strong. Then we place the *cimbra* on top of the beams. That forms a platform strong enough to receive a *colado* this deep." He holds his hands about four inches apart, one above the other.

"Once the concrete is dry, we'll remove the beams from below," adds Francisco. "Then we'll pull the boards off—and there's our new ceiling."

Rick pictures the results. The *colado,* the layer of concrete, will make a lid for the box they've built out of bricks and mortar. It will be flush with the concrete roof of the living room. *Seems simple enough,* he thinks. *But first we have to haul all the stuff.*

It takes several hours—two dozen trips apiece—before the heap on the corner is gone and a new heap has accumulated in the Romeros' courtyard. The job tires Rick faster than he expected, not just because it's hard work but also because he knows that finishing *this* task will simply lead to another: fitting all the separate beams and boards into place. Only the thought of calling Ellen distracts him enough to keep him going.

The Romeros have no phone. None of their neighbors has one, either. There's a *bodega,* though, a little grocery store on Calle Aparicio, where he can make a local call. After lunch, he tells Julio that he wants to buy some chocolate, then races down Callejón Hidalgo as fast as possible. He'd tried calling once before, but Ellen wasn't home, and he'd decided not to leave a message on the answering machine. Maybe today he'll get lucky.

In the *bodega,* Rick pops some coins into a pay phone and dials the number Ellen gave him. The line rings with a loud tone.

"¿Bueno?" asks a woman's voice.

"Quisiera hablar con Ellen, por favor," Rick says. I wish to speak with Ellen, please. It occurs to him that he doesn't even know her last name.

There's a brief silence. Rick can hear footsteps fading. Then others, faster and noisier than the first ones, grow quickly louder.

"Hello?" says a familiar voice.

"Ellen, it's Rick." There's no response. "Rick Dresner. We met in the park—"

"Hey! Yeah, I remember you!"

He's pleased that she sounds so friendly. "I wanted to call and say hi."

"Cool—I'm glad you did."

"How's it going?"

"Fine, I guess. Sorta boring."

"Maybe we could get together," Rick says quickly.

Somewhere in the background there's a big splash. "I'd like that," Ellen replies.

"Great! How about at the *jardín?*"

"The what?"

"The *jardín.* The park where we met."

Another pause. Rick can hear a male voice in the background. He can't understand the words, but he can tell that the man is speaking English. "Well, there's just one problem," says Ellen. "My dad doesn't really like me wandering around by myself."

"*I'd* be with you."

"Right, but still—he wants to meet you first. So could you come here?"

"Sure. No problem."

"Maybe for lunch?"

"Sounds great."

"We have a swimming pool."

An image comes to him—Ellen in a bathing suit, the two of them splashing around in the pool. "Terrific," he says.

"How about Wednesday?"

Rick is disappointed. Today is Thursday; he'll have to wait nearly a week to see Ellen. But he doesn't have much choice. "That's fine with me," he says. Then right away he wonders what

Julio and Emiliana have scheduled for next Wednesday. And whatever they have planned, how he'll manage to get away alone.

"Hang on." Ellen's voice is muffled as she calls out to someone. Then she's back on the line. "All right. Let's say . . . noon?"

"I'll be there."

She gives him directions. "See you then."

Returning to the Romeros', Rick feels both delighted and frustrated—delighted because Ellen seemed so friendly; frustrated because it's six whole days till Wednesday. How will he wait that long? He wants to see her *now*.

Oddly enough, he discovers that the call to Ellen has energized him, that he can concentrate better than before. Helping Julio and Francisco set up the beam-and-board supports gives him a sense of purpose even though the work is hard.

Both Julio and Francisco take notice. *"Estás trabajando a gusto,"* Julio tells him. You're doing just great.

Rick grins. Little does Julio know *why* he's doing great. He raises both arms and flexes his biceps like a muscleman. "Come on! Let's throw these boards together," he shouts. "Let's build this house!"

El Colado

The next day, Julio assembles the bag of tools, the shovels, the garden hose, and the stack of square metal *botes* he'd borrowed from his friend. It's time to tackle the *colado*. This will require a great deal of effort, so he has called in reinforcements. Alfonso, Lucho, and Rodolfo will pitch in, which will earn them a meal and a small payment. Hilaria will help Emiliana assist the men. The two younger boys and their little sister arrive on time. Half an hour passes before Rodolfo shows up, his own "tools" in hand—a beach towel, a folding aluminum chair, and a guitar. It's as if he's visiting the seaside rather than a construction site.

"¡*Ya llegó el conjunto!*" says Julio. Here comes the band!

Rodolfo fends off the taunt. "*Hola, Tío. ¿Listos para bailar?*" Hi, Uncle. Ready to dance?

"Yeah, right," says Julio. "Come on, guys, grab your shovels."

"Shovels?" Rick mutters in English. Somehow he had fooled himself into believing that they wouldn't be mixing concrete the old-fashioned way. Surely some kind of machine would rescue them from this awful task. But no. As with every other job they've taken on, they'll use only their own muscle power.

Following Julio's directions, they dump loads of sand, crushed rock, and cement into a pile that soon takes up the middle third of the courtyard. Then he scrambles to the top and, using his shovel, carves a crater big enough so that the heap looks like a volcano. He slides down, raising a cloud of dust, Alfonso turns on the tap, and Lucho aims the garden hose at the crater and starts filling it with water.

Alfonso pulls a bright red bandana from his pocket and ties it over his mouth and nose. Francisco does the same. Julio takes out two and hands one to Rick. They look like a band of masked *bandidos*.

"¡*Ya!*" says Julio. Now!

At this signal, the *bandidos* attack the pile with their shovels. The noise is much louder than Rick expected—the clack and clank of steel against chunks of stone. The work is harder, too. He thought this new task would be like mixing mortar, but the mass of sand, cement, and crushed rock feels heavier and is much more ungainly, with the stones repeatedly resisting or deflecting his shovel blade. It doesn't help that they have to work fast; the stream of water runs off the pile unless the men combine it quickly with the materials. Grunting and muttering, they stab furiously at the pile as if trying to kill a monstrous amoeba.

Alfonso and Julio are especially energetic as they turn over globs of concrete. Rick quickly tires and works more slowly. Then a pall of dust penetrates his bandana and drives him, gasping, away from the pile.

The others gradually reduce the volcano to a lower, darker, wetter mass. The shovels keep clanking against the rocks, but now they also make a sucking noise as they leave the mixture. Rick rejoins the effort and discovers that during his brief time on the sidelines, the stuff has changed consistency. It's now even heavier than before—a shovelful weighs probably fifteen or twenty pounds. He can scarcely believe that Julio and the others can lift big blobs of it so easily.

He's relieved when Julio announces, *"Listo."* Ready. At once Francisco sets aside his shovel, turns to the stack of *botes,* and starts passing them around.

Rick takes one and waits his turn while Alfonso fills some of the others. Each *bote* holds about five big shovelfuls of concrete. When his *bote* is full, Rick hefts it and is appalled to discover how heavy it is—sixty pounds, at least, maybe even seventy-five or eighty—so heavy that lifting it to his shoulder, not to mention carrying it up a temporary ramp to the top of the new room, will be difficult. He tries not to panic. How will he manage more than a dozen trips?

What really upsets him is that Rodolfo, who is the biggest guy present, has stepped in and grabbed the easiest job—filling the *botes*—while he and Francisco and Alfonso are stuck carrying the concrete. Julio will stay on the roof and settle the concrete into place as his helpers bring it up one *bote* at a time. Rick has no argument with that; Julio is the expert. But it bothers him that Rodolfo has given himself such an easy ride. And Lucho, who is obviously muscular and fit, just stands around watching. Will they rotate tasks? Maybe. But no one has said anything about that, so Rick isn't sure, and he doesn't want to make an issue of it and risk offending the two guys—and, more important, Julio and Francisco.

After a while, Rick finds a good work rhythm. His arms and legs grow accustomed to the effort of hoisting a full *bote* to his shoulder, climbing carefully up the ramp, and dumping the load of concrete where Julio directs him. He doesn't even mind when Rodolfo turns over his job to Lucho, sits down on his folding chair, and contributes only by strumming his guitar and singing. Rodolfo has a pleasant tenor voice, and the melody he sings somehow makes the job easier.

They mix a second load of concrete in the courtyard. By now Rick's arms no longer fully control the shovel he holds, and his hands shake when he pauses briefly to rest. The work grows more and more difficult as the day advances and the temperature rises, but there's no stopping. The crew has to move fast, before the concrete hardens.

Time after time Lucho fills the *bote* with concrete. Time after time Rick hoists it and climbs the ramp. Time after time he dumps the load, which falls with a loud slopping noise onto the boards.

Each trip feels harder and more painful than the one before. His back and shoulders throb. His hands grow so slick with sweat that just keeping a grip on the *bote* is a struggle. His feet don't seem reliable now, and sometimes he nearly trips.

Then, abruptly, they're done. Rick reaches the roof with a *bote* full of concrete only to have Julio wave him off. "No more?" he asks, confused.

"Terminado," Julio announces. Finished. He stands, and his tendons make a loud noise, like snapping twigs, as he straightens. A large expanse of slate-gray concrete, a rectangle about twelve feet wide and sixteen feet long, lies before him. Though visibly exhausted, he looks pleased with their efforts. *"Está a todo dar,"* he says. It's great.

Rick is thrilled. They did it!

The men laugh, hug, and slap one another on the back.

At that moment, fifteen or twenty pigeons that ordinarily roost in the *pirul* tree next to the Romeros' house take off from the branches and fly over to the new *colado*. They land and pace frantically back and forth over the still-wet concrete, leaving their little Y-shaped footprints all over its surface.

Wetbacks

"Ricardo, there's someone here to see you," Julio announces Saturday morning when Rick is at the breakfast table. For a moment, Rick thinks that Ellen has shown up to visit him, and he leaps to his feet. But his excitement fades at once. She doesn't even know where he lives! Besides, Julio is already ushering a man into the kitchen. "I'd like you to meet my brother," he says.

Rick reaches out to shake hands with the guest. *So this is the infamous Juan,* he thinks as he sizes up the man before him. Juan is actually a few inches taller than Julio, yet he lacks his brother's energy and wiry build. His face is lumpy. His teeth are brown and diseased. But beyond this, it's the mussed-up, dirty clothes, the hunched shoulders, the hat held meekly before him, that make him look small.

"Señor Dresner, I am Juan Romero," he says. Then he bows, adding, "At your service."

Embarrassed by the man's excessive politeness, Rick nods. "I'm glad to meet you."

"No, the pleasure is entirely mine," Juan continues. "Truly a great honor."

Julio retreats to the doorway. "Juan wants to discuss something with you," he says, and he leaves at once.

Why did he go? Rick wonders. *And where are Emiliana and Francisco? Why aren't they gathering the way they do when other family members arrive?*

Rick offers Juan a chair, and they sit face-to-face with only the table between them. A sour smell wafts toward Rick. Whiskey? Tequila? It's *maybe* eight o'clock, but the man has already been drinking.

"I hate to bother you, for I know you're busy," Juan states. Then his tone changes abruptly. "But I need your help. Because of my great family obligations—our Lord has blessed me with many children—I have no alternative but to travel *al norte.* I must seek employment there." He lifts a hand as if to hold back the inevitable objections. "Not among *los mojados,* but rather as a documented worker."

Rick nods. He's not sure where the conversation is going, but he understands what Juan is referring to. *Mojados* means "wetbacks," a slang term for people who cross the Rio Grande to enter the United States illegally.

Juan hesitates, then reaches into his denim jacket. He pulls out a laminated green card and pushes it across the table toward Rick. The card bears a blurry black-and-white photo of Juan. The words, printed in English, say something about permission to work in the United States for a certain period of time.

Looking it over, Rick says, "It sounds like you've got everything organized."

Juan nods gloomily.

"When do you leave?"

"As soon as possible." Juan glances at the document, then at Rick. "Does this look . . . you know . . . authentic?"

The word hits Rick like a slap. The entry card must be counterfeit, and Juan is asking his opinion of its appearance. He gestures in bafflement and shakes his head. "I have no idea!" he exclaims, his voice louder than he intends.

Juan seems equally baffled. "But do you *think* it looks authentic?"

"Señor Romero," Rick says, "I've never seen one of these cards before."

"But you're *americano.*"

"That doesn't mean I know anything about this stuff," Rick says. He's touched that Juan would consider him some kind of expert, and saddened by the man's desperation. At the same time, he's annoyed to be put in a position of trying to help him break the law.

Juan looks crestfallen. He holds the laminated card in both hands and pretends to contemplate the writing there.

Impulsively, Rick asks, "Where did you get it?"

"From someone I know."

"Did he charge you for it?"

"Of course!" Juan looks up, as if startled that anyone could ask such a question. "Three thousand pesos."

Rick does a quick calculation. That's a lot of money—a fortune for someone like Juan. He wants to tell him he's been scammed, but he fights the impulse and says only, "I see."

They sit for a moment in silence. "Well," Juan says at last, "I thank you greatly."

"I'm sorry," Rick replies.

"On the contrary—it is I who should apologize for troubling you."

They stand and shake hands formally; then Juan leaves.

Emiliana appears soon after, as if she'd been waiting for Juan's departure, and Rick tells her about the conversation.

"There's a custom here of traveling *al norte*," she says. "Sometimes women do it, but mostly it's the men. Young men, even boys. I suppose a few of them see it as a big adventure, but most people just need the money. There's not enough work here, so they go *al norte*." Her tone is irritable, almost contemptuous.

"You don't approve," Rick says.

She glances at him, smiling, but there's a glint of anger in her eyes. "Ricardo, it's very, very dangerous." She draws out each word: *"muy . . . muy . . . peligroso."*

"Then wouldn't it be better if they did something else?" he asks.

"Like what?" She gestures with both hands, palms upward and empty.

"Maybe they could work in some other Mexican town or city."

"Ricardo, *where?* There's no work! And we can't earn enough to survive on Mexican wages, anyway."

"But is it really worth the risk?"

"Listen. About ten years ago, my mother got sick. Kidney problems, liver problems. We took her to the hospital, and the doctors saved her life. But a week's medical expenses added up to more than Julio made in a year. What were we to do? Julio told me, 'I'll go find work in Texas.' I pleaded with him to stay, but he wouldn't listen. He's very loyal. He felt it was his duty to support his family, no matter what. So he went."

"Knowing don Julio," Rick says, "I'm sure it was a big adventure."

Again that smile. "For Julio, *everything* is a big adventure."

"It turned out all right, didn't it?"

"Thanks to God's mercy," she says. "But it doesn't always. You should hear the stories that people around here tell. About husbands who travel *al norte* and never come back. About sons and daughters who get lost in the desert and die of thirst. About girls who get raped or murdered."

Rick feels sick to his stomach. He's read news stories about the dangers that border crossers encounter, but it's totally different to think about someone he knows facing those dangers. "What about Francisco?" he asks. "Has he ever wanted to go? And what about the other men in the family?"

Emiliana makes the sign of the cross, a gesture that seems matter-of-fact rather than dramatic. "My prayers for Francisco have been answered. He has never wanted to work in *el norte*. And if he gets accepted into the teachers' college, maybe he'll never have to. As for the others, that's a different matter. A couple of our nephews have gone, and so far they've been spared the worst. But Juan—now *there's* someone who's destined for trouble. That man has nothing but bad luck. Sooner or later he'll come to grief." Emiliana shakes her head. "To tell you the truth, Juan will come to grief whether he stays or goes," she says in disgust. "He'll come to grief even if he spends the rest of his life sitting at his kitchen table."

Apprenticeship

When the *colado* is dry, Julio and Rick start work on the second-story rooms. Francisco isn't always around, because he has taken a part-time job at SuperTienda, a little supermarket in town—a decision that surprises Rick. Why isn't he continuing with *la obra*? His absence slows them down. Fortunately, Rick's bricklaying skills keep improving, so they still make good headway. Julio seems pleased. His chief concern is that the rainy season will start soon. It's late July now, and so far the summer has been dry. That's a lucky break, because anything more than a few showers could damage the work in progress. Now they just need their luck to hold.

Following Julio's instructions, Rick begins work on the back wall, an unbroken expanse of bricks facing Juan and Antonia's house next door. Julio will work on the other walls, a more difficult task because they have to accommodate several windows.

Rick feels comfortable with this arrangement. He knows that his technique isn't good enough for him to go ahead without supervision, but that's part of what he enjoys—Julio's proximity. They're working both together and apart.

Julio lays the bricks with an ease that Rick finds both impressive and instructive. There is no wasted motion. He slaps down a mass of mortar, settles a *tabique* into place, and trims the excess mortar that squeezes out from between the bricks. Simply watching him helps Rick improve his technique. And now and then, Julio checks up on him—walks over, sizes up how he's doing, and offers a few suggestions. He never criticizes; he simply points things out. "That's great," he'll say, "but try the edge of the trowel rather than the tip." Or he'll suggest alternatives. "I think that dark *tabique* is a better size than the yellowish one."

At some point, Rick realizes how much he's enjoying himself. Bricklaying isn't easy, and he isn't sure how well he's doing it. But he feels good—strong despite the demands on his body, comfortable despite the hot sun, and happy to be working with his friends. He and Julio don't talk much when it's just the two of them, and their few words focus on bricks, mortar, plumb lines, and trowels. Yet at times he feels as close to Julio as he does to his own father. The situation is more complex when Francisco is around, because the balance of the relationship changes. But it's still comfortable, and Rick enjoys joking around with someone his own age.

He keeps working on the wall. All the while the sounds of Santo Domingo—the barking dogs, the distant blaring radios, the honking cars, the crowing roosters, the shouting kids, and the tolling church bells—waft up from the town below, each noise diminished by distance and time. He daydreams about Ellen. He wonders idly how his parents and friends are doing. But none of these thoughts linger. He feels nearly hypnotized by the rhythm of his work in this setting. At the same time, he feels fully present in each moment, fully alive.

Comidas Típicas

"I don't like those pigeons," Julio says at breakfast Monday morning. "They're ruining our work."

Emiliana hands him a plate of pancakes, eggs, and sausage. "No, they aren't," she tells him.

Francisco comes to his dad's defense. "They're a nuisance. Let's get rid of them."

"They walked on the *colado*," states Julio, leaning toward his wife. "They put footprints all over it. They'll do it next time, too."

"So?"

"So—" Julio turns to Rick and smiles broadly. "How can I impress our guest with my fine work if there are footprints all over it?"

The truth is, lots of pigeons live on the Romeros' property. They gather on the tile roofs, pacing and preening, and they descend—a whirlwind of wings, claws, and beaks—whenever anyone accidentally drops food on the ground. But mostly they roost in the *pirul* tree, dozens of them among the reddish-brown branches.

Rick considers them a minor nuisance—annoying when they flutter about on the patio but harmless otherwise. He isn't entirely sure what Julio has against them.

That afternoon, while working on the second-story walls, Julio reaches out and grabs two of the birds from their perch on a nearby limb. "*Son muy mansitos,*" he announces. They're tame little guys. Then he holds them out for Rick and Francisco to see.

Even from where he stands in the courtyard below, Rick can tell how docile the pigeons are. They rest in Julio's hands, looking around stupidly. "What will you do with them?" he asks.

"Bring me the crow's cage."

Francisco, who has been mixing mortar in the courtyard, picks up the green metal birdcage, climbs the ramp, and sets it down near Julio. Rick follows, curious about what will happen next.

"Open it for me," Julio says. He waits for Francisco to pull open the wire door, then shoves both birds inside. They flutter about for a moment before alighting on the wooden crosspiece. Julio looks pleased. "New pets for Emiliana."

He reaches over to the *pirul* and grabs another pigeon. There's no struggle, and in a moment it's captive with the other two.

Amused, Rick decides to try his luck. He reaches up and takes hold of a bird. It twists slightly in his hand but otherwise makes no fuss. The only commotion comes from Tizón and Sombra, who bark frantically in the courtyard. Rick crouches, shoving the pigeon into the cage.

Francisco catches three more. *"¡Qué pichones tan estúpidos!"* he mutters. What stupid pigeons!

Seven birds are now captive—so many that the cage seems a solid mass of feathers. The pigeons fight for position on the crosspiece. There's no room for all of them, and when one falls off, it squabbles with the others to regain its place. Pecking and clawing one another, the birds struggle constantly.

"I guess Emiliana should start making some *mole*," says Julio.

Rick doesn't get it at first. *Mole* is a complex sauce that Mexicans use on meat. Rick has eaten *puerco en mole*—pork in *mole*. And he's eaten *guajalote en mole*—turkey in *mole*. But he has never heard of *pichones en mole*. He tries to guess if Julio is serious or not. To his dismay, Julio picks up the birdcage and heads toward the kitchen.

"Emiliana, look!" Julio calls out. "Look what we caught!"

That night, Emiliana and Hilaria set to work in the kitchen. They grind spices with a black stone mortar and pestle. They cook vegetables, chiles, bananas, nuts, and raisins. They mix everything in a big copper pot that simmers on the burner, releasing an aroma that's sweet and spicy at the same time.

Rick reminds himself that he's an adventurous eater. On this trip, he's tried quite a few new things: roast goat, fried cactus leaves, squash soup, barbecued piglet . . . But *pichones*? Pigeons caught right off the tree? He can't believe that Emiliana will cook such a bizarre dish.

"Quiero que pruebes nuestras comidas típicas," she tells him. I'd like you to try our local dishes.

What can he say? He'll be busy at dinnertime tomorrow? He's allergic to pigeon? His religion forbids him to eat small birds? He decides not to push his luck. He doesn't want to offend his hosts—especially not Emiliana, who has worked many hours making the *mole* in which the pigeons will meet their doom.

The next morning, Rick notices that one of the pigeons has developed some kind of sore at the base of its beak. A gross-looking gooey red blob protrudes near its right eye. Rick stares at it for a while. Then he sees that several other pigeons have ugly sores on their heads, too. Yesterday he had no appetite for *mole de pichón;* now this feeling turns to revulsion.

He fetches Emiliana from the kitchen. Hilaria has already arrived for the day and trails after them.

"I think you should see this," he says, pointing to the cage. "The birds don't look so great."

Emiliana peers into the cage. She prods the pigeons with her right index finger, startling them, then waits for them to settle and peers again. *"¿Qué será?"* What can it be?

"¿Están enfermos?" asks Hilaria. Are they sick?

"I don't know. It could be because they're pecking each other."

"Pobrecitos," says Emiliana. Poor little things.

Rick's hopes rise. If she feels sorry for them, maybe she'll spare them altogether. "Maybe they caught rabies," he tells her.

Although he meant the comment to be a joke, Emiliana looks concerned. "Can birds catch rabies?"

"I don't know."

"I suppose it's possible," she says. Moving so close that her nose almost touches the cage, she stares at the captives.

Rick isn't sure what to say. He doesn't really believe that pigeons can catch rabies. At the same time, he's so grossed out by the possibility of eating *mole de pichón* that he doesn't want to talk Emiliana out of her worries.

"I've heard of something called *la viruela*," she says.

"*La viruela*," echoes Hilaria ominously.

Rick has no idea what *la viruela* might be, but it sounds terrible. "Could that be what they've got?" he asks. "I mean, is that what pigeons catch?"

Emiliana doesn't answer. She just gazes somberly at the frightened creatures. Then she opens the wire door and starts pulling out pigeons. "*¡Adiós, pichones! ¡Adiós!*" she declares, tossing them in the air one by one. "We'll use the *mole* for something else."

The birds take off with a clatter of wings.

"*¡Adiós, adiós, adiós!*"

Rain

They spend the day building the upper rooms. Julio and Francisco tackle the outer walls, while Rick concentrates on the back wall again. By now he feels confident about his technique. The mortar goes down just right. The *tabiques* settle easily into place. Each row is level and neat.

Looking up from his work late in the afternoon, Rick notices that the weather is deteriorating. Thunderheads rise to the west—slate gray in the middle, brilliant white at the edges. Massive curtains of rain, maybe two or three miles wide and ten miles distant, hang over the desert and obscure the mountains beyond. Soon the sky is almost black.

"*¡Ya merito!*" shouts Julio. Any moment now! He and Francisco and Rick scramble to drape, and anchor, big sheets of plastic over the half-finished walls. Then the rain begins to fall.

Rick watches the storm sweep across the sky. He's only half-aware of how wet he's getting, until Emiliana, who has been monitoring the situation from below, scolds her husband: "Don Julio, tell the boys to stop. Our guest will get sick!"

Rick puts away his tools and joins the family in the kitchen. Emiliana serves everyone beans, rice, and thick homemade tortillas. It's a far more basic meal than usual—no meat, no vegetables—which puzzles him. But he's too hungry to think about the situation further.

Throughout the meal, Rick listens to the sound of rain hitting the tile roof above them. It's a pleasant sound, calming after a hard day's work. The smell of wet earth pleases him, too. He feels comfortable and happy. Yet the Romeros seem tense. Now and then they all stop eating and listen. Belatedly, Rick realizes what they're worried about. Will the roof hold, or will it leak?

For a while, there's no problem. Then, just as everyone begins to relax, large drops slip through the clay tiles overhead.

Julio shoves his plate away. He's smiling, but Rick can tell he's annoyed. "Well, how about that!" he exclaims. "I thought we'd have no problem."

They joke about the situation for a while, perhaps to ease the tension, perhaps to ward off bad luck. But soon drops turn into trickles, and water, brown with dirt from the roof, spatters furniture, people, and everything else in the kitchen.

"What are we going to do?" Francisco asks.

"Well, guess," Julio snaps—one of the few times that Rick has heard him sound annoyed by his son.

Working quickly, the four of them remove all food items from the kitchen. They consolidate the furniture and drape it with plastic. They unplug the fridge and drape it, too. The noise of the storm increases. The scent of wet earth grows stronger, until the kitchen smells like a cave. Runnels stream down everywhere. Water pools on the floor, flows out the doorway, and spills down the steps into the courtyard. In the *pirul* tree, wet pigeons sit clumped together, fluffing themselves and poking at their feathers.

Taletelling

Rick and the Romeros flee to the living room and settle there. At least it's dry—that's all anyone cares about at the moment.

"*Ay, Dios mío,*" groans Emiliana. Oh, my god. "What a disaster."

Julio smiles. "Ah, well, what's a little rain? We're fine so long as the new walls don't get too wet."

Yet the setback clearly affects everyone. It's only eight o'clock, too early for bed, but no one seems to have much energy left.

"You want to hear a story about a rainy night?" Julio asks Rick. He leans close, as if to reveal a secret that he doesn't want the others to hear. "Once I worked at a ranch where there was a *nahual*. I was young then, and *nahuales* try harder to get you if you're young."

"What's a *nahual*?" Rick asks.

"A *nahual* is someone who makes a pact with the devil. In exchange for selling his soul and vowing to live a wicked life, the *nahual* gains the ability to take the form of an animal—a dog, a wolf, a crow, a cat, a mountain lion—so he can disguise himself while doing evil deeds. Or else he takes no form at all, so he can fly through the air and walk through walls. Lots of people out there in the ranchos have become *nahuales*."

"Don Julio," says Emiliana. "Don't scare Ricardo."

"I'm not scaring him."

"You are."

"Am I scaring you?" Julio asks, raising his right eyebrow.

"No. Keep going," Rick says. This is like listening to a ghost story at summer camp—only a Mexican version.

"*¿Ya ves?*" See? Julio smiles triumphantly at his wife.

Francisco watches his parents, looking patient rather than amused. "Papi—"

"Anyway," says Julio, "once there was a wild rainstorm like this one. I woke up terrified in the middle of the night. I didn't know what had frightened me, but I'd never been so scared in my life. Then I saw it. A *nahual*! It was pressing against my neck, so hard I could barely breathe. I couldn't speak, couldn't even gasp. I twisted my head away so it couldn't look me in the eyes, but there it was—on the other side of me!"

Julio pauses to bulge both eyes and make a horrified grimace.

"Papi—"

"I managed to put my Saint Ignatius medal in my mouth, just as you're supposed to, and this protected me a little. It also forced the *nahual* to speak. Not words, but a hiss, like wind. *Ssa . . . ssa . . . ssa . . . ssa . . . ssa!* I said, 'I know who you are; you're the devil's henchman! But you don't frighten me! Jesus Christ protects me, and all the saints in heaven, too! Go bother someone else!' I was still frightened, but I didn't let it know that."

Francisco and Emiliana glance at each other, but neither interrupts Julio's story.

"The demon did nothing! Then I knew how weak it was, and it knew *I* knew, and it left and never came back."

Julio looks hard at his listeners, perhaps detecting their skepticism. "You don't believe me? Okay, don't believe me. Say it was only a trick of the rain. Think whatever you like. *I* know what I saw."

When he falls silent, the only sound comes from the wind nudging the door. The flame flutters from the candle like a torn flag. No one moves.

"There's no such thing as a *nahual.*" It's Francisco. Sitting straight in his chair, he speaks without looking at his father.

"I saw the *nahual,*" says Julio. "I heard it."

"There's no such thing."

"With my own eyes and ears, Francisco."

"You saw something, but not a *nahual.*"

"It really was." Julio's voice grows urgent.

"That's just a superstition," Francisco states emphatically. "It's a silly idea—really *nopaluda.*"

Nopaluda is a word Rick hasn't heard before, so it takes a moment for him to figure out what it means. *"Nopal"* he knows—it's a flat-leafed cactus—and *"-uda"* turns the noun into an adjective. So Francisco has called Julio's tale "cactusy." He is essentially accusing his father of being a hick, a country bumpkin.

This comment seems to stun Julio and Emiliana. Rick is shocked, too, having grown accustomed to Francisco's obvious respect for his parents.

"Are you calling your father a liar?" asks Emiliana. Although she speaks in a calm voice, she gazes intently at her son.

Francisco doesn't meet her gaze. "No," he says quickly. "What I meant is, things aren't always what they seem."

"I heard the wailing," Julio says. "I felt the *nahual* pressing against my face."

"I'm not denying that," Francisco says, holding his ground. "But what you saw and heard doesn't mean there was a *nahual* in the room. It doesn't mean that *nahuales* exist."

Julio smiles defiantly, his gold tooth glimmering in the candlelight. "What was it, then?"

"I don't know. Something else. An illusion."

"That demon pulling the life out of me was an illusion? Hah!" Julio's eyes glisten. "Son, there really are *nahuales*. You'll believe me when one gets hold of you some night."

There's an awkward silence, then Emiliana intervenes. "Ay, don Julio." She sighs. "This is too confusing for me. I don't know what to think anymore." She turns to Rick. "If you like scary stories—really scary ones—then ask don Julio to tell you about his trips to Texas."

Rick feels cornered. He's tired. He wants to sleep. But he can hardly go to bed with everyone in the living room. "I'd love to know what happened," he says.

Los Mojados

"You know why we cross the border?" asks Julio. "Because there's not enough work here. And the pay *en el norte* is better. Some of the ranchers even give us food." He sits back, more relaxed now, content to be telling another tale. "I've been to Texas three times. Most of the men in Santo Domingo have been *al norte* at least once. My nephew Rafael, Aniseto's son, just got back. He didn't like it there, and he didn't earn much money. But I like the wages, so I keep going back.

"Here's how we make the trip. First we take a bus north, or else the train. We get off near one of the border towns. We don't have papers, so we have to cross over at night. Usually a lot of *mojados* are waiting by the river. If the water is low, we try to cross by ourselves. If the water is high, we have to pay someone to take us over. There are guys called coyotes who charge a fee for that. Some have boats. Or else they string a rope across, and you follow the rope from one shore to the other side.

"Some coyotes will take you across the border by truck— drive you right to the ranches and farms where Americans will hire you. I've never done that. Riding in a truck full of *mojados* is a good way to get spotted by *la migra*—the border police. Besides, many of the coyotes are crooks. They take your money and tell you they'll give you a ride, but they only drive you a short distance from the river and then leave you in the middle of nowhere. Or they turn you over to corrupt officers in *la migra* who pay the coyotes a kickback. Once I heard about some *mojados* who got a ride in a sealed cargo truck. The coyote must have gotten scared—maybe he thought *la migra* was about to catch him—so he abandoned the truck in the desert. The *mojados* couldn't get out. The temperature out there gets very hot, and it must have been even hotter inside the truck. Everyone died."

Rick notices Emiliana looking at him. She nods, as if to ask, "Do you believe me now?"

"A boat is probably safer," Julio continues, "and of course you don't get wet. But I've heard that *la migra* have a plane that flies up and down the river, and if they see a boat crossing, they'll lower a rope with a hook and flip it over. Sometimes there are men in Jeeps patrolling the other side—men with machine guns. I've never used a boat to cross. I probably would have, but I never had the chance.

"So I just waded across, at night. I took off most of my clothes—everything but my shorts!—and held them in a pile on my head while we crossed. The first time the river was low; it only came up to my chest. So it wasn't too hard to get to the other side.

"My brother Juan was along that time. Also my friend Miguel the Stringbean and a guy nicknamed the Turkey. Miguel couldn't swim, and he lost his footing and nearly got carried away. But we all managed to get across, and we started walking.

"You know how long we walked? Six days and six nights. Each of us had only a little food. We couldn't go near the towns, since *la migra* would catch us, and out in the desert there's no one to help you. We walked and walked. My knees hurt, but we walked and walked. We had to get deeper into Texas, where the farms and ranches are. The heat was very bad, so bad that the land looked soft, like it was melting. Miguel the Stringbean was having a hard time. He'd sprained his back when he lost his balance in the river, and he kept thinking about the fact that he'd almost drowned.

"We came to a high barbed-wire fence. Three of us climbed it—no big deal. Miguel was so tired that he decided to crawl under it. There was a wheat field on the other side. He couldn't see what he was getting into, and when he was still crouched down, a rattlesnake bit him on the nose. Right on the nose! He died in about five minutes. We scraped a hole for him and buried him as best we could."

"Oh, my god! That's terrible!" Rick exclaims.

"Yes," Julio says simply. "We were lucky to reach a melon farm soon after that. The owner fed us and gave us some clothes. We harvested melons for several months. Then one day a truck pulled up when we were washing up by the windmill, and it was *la migra*."

"At least you made it home," says Emiliana when Julio pauses.

"True."

"For a while, I wasn't so sure I'd ever see you again."

"Well, God protected me."

Emiliana shakes her head, as if doubting even God's ability to preserve Julio from misfortune.

"I went off to Texas again a few years later," says Julio. "My luck was better that time. We took the train—Juan, Alfonso, Jorge Escobar, the Turkey, and me. We didn't have trouble crossing the river, but the heat was terrible. We ran out of food in a few days. We had nothing to drink but the water we found in muddy ditches. We walked day and night, day and night, and we kept getting lost because the heat drove us half-crazy.

"One morning, we saw two men sitting under a mesquite tree in the distance. Were they *la migra*? After a while, we crept closer and saw that they were Mexicans. We waved and yelled. No answer. We walked over to them and said, 'Hey, *compadres,* how's it going?' But they were dead—all dried up like mummies, sitting there in the shade with their mouths wide open."

"Ay, Don Julio," mutters Emiliana. "May God have mercy."

Rick shakes his head. It sounds like a scene from a horror movie. "What did you do?" he asks.

"Did you bury them?" Francisco chimes in.

"We didn't have the strength," Julio replies. "And after another day, we almost *were* them. We just wanted to sit down and die because we couldn't take the heat and thirst any longer. So we walked until we reached a highway. We didn't care if we got arrested. We stood in the road and flagged down a pickup. We thought the driver was *la migra,* since he was a huge gringo with rifles in the back of his truck.

"He was only a rancher. 'You need work?' he asked. Of course we did! What did he think—maybe we were out in the desert for a hike? He took us to his chicken farm. He was a good boss. He paid us well, and there was a big wooden house that we could sleep in. We made lots of money, but *la migra* found us after a few months. Perhaps they saw us from one of those airplanes that fly back and forth to look for *mojados.* Anyway, they came to the ranch, and we took off into a field. One of them shouted, 'Stop, or we'll shoot!' We stopped when we heard that. They treat you okay if you don't run, so we didn't run. 'All right, boys,' he said. 'Let's get you back to Mexico.' "

"*¿Ya ves?*" exclaims Emiliana. "He goes, he gets caught, he comes back. So tell me. What's the point?"

"I earned some money," Julio says proudly.

"True."

"And we needed it."

"Also true."

"So that's the point." He pauses and leans back in his chair. Then he goes on. "The third time I went was when we needed money to pay for Emiliana's mother's medicines. Fine—I didn't mind going. Two other guys and I went together, and the crossing was okay. We found work and made a lot of money. Then, of course, we got caught. We always get caught. *La migra* took us away in a bus we call the kennel since it has chicken wire across the windows like a cage for dogs. They drove us to Laredo and put us in jail."

"In jail!" Rick exclaims.

Julio nods. "They wanted to make sure we were only little fish. The big fish are the people who fake papers and the coyotes who smuggle people across the border. That's who they really want to catch. Anyway, they treated us pretty well, those *migra*. They gave each of us a towel and some soap when we arrived, so we could take a shower. They fed us three times a day on metal trays with dividers. And everyone got his own bed, even though the place was crowded.

"You've never seen so many *mojados*! Sometimes fights broke out, since there's a lot of taunting and mocking among the men. Nobody got hurt too badly, though, because when you come, they take away your knife and your belt. They take away your money, too, but this is what I couldn't believe: later, they actually gave me back every cent they'd taken! I had to use part of it for a bus ticket. Some of the men there didn't have any money, and they had to stay in jail. I had money, so after a few days, they put me on a bus, and I came home."

"That must have been a big relief," says Rick. "After all you'd been through . . . "

"Actually, it wasn't so bad in jail—not as bad as some of the ranches I've worked on," says Julio. "At least the beds didn't have bedbugs."

Muddy Waters

"Ay, don Julio. You can't be serious," Emiliana says when he finishes his story.

"Why shouldn't I be serious?"

"To say it's fine just because there weren't any bedbugs!"

"Well, there weren't."

"It's still a terrible thing, those Americans locking you up."

Rick suddenly feels uncomfortable, as if Emiliana were holding him—the only gringo present—partly responsible for what happened to Julio.

"That's just how it goes," Julio says, gesturing with both palms open. "My job is to find work—"

"They shouldn't arrest Mexicans just for wanting work," she cuts in.

"—and their job is to stop me."

In a way, Rick understands Emiliana's outrage more than Julio's acceptance. Julio has told his stories without expressing anger, frustration, or even annoyance. It's almost as if he's described events that happened to someone else. Is he really so matter-of-fact about his trips to Texas? Or is this his way of protecting himself from memories of the hardships he's faced?

"Let's hear what Ricardo has to say," Emiliana suggests cheerfully.

There's a sweet smile on her face, but Rick wonders if she's set a trap for him. He's heard all the pronouncements about illegal workers and immigrants from politicians, citizens, and human rights groups back home, and he has no intention of wading into those muddy waters. "I'm just glad," he says, "that don Julio got home safely."

Emiliana seems to recognize that he's trying to weasel out of an argument. "But what do you *believe*—"

"You know what I believe?" Francisco says quickly. "I believe it's getting late." He glances at his watch. "Even later than I thought."

Rick understands that Francisco is trying to rescue him, and he's grateful.

Sighing, Emiliana looks at her husband.

"We have lots to do tomorrow," says Julio.

"Well, then," she says, getting up. "Off to bed, everyone!"

The truth, Rick tells himself as he flops onto the sofa a short while later, is that he doesn't know what to think about this issue—but there has to be a better solution than the endless cat-and-mouse game between *los mojados* and *la migra*.

He rolls over. Right now, what he really wants to think about is Ellen. He wonders what tomorrow will be like, what her family will be like, and whether she's wondering about him. At last he falls asleep.

La Colonia Americana

"I'm going to go get my camera fixed," Rick tells Julio late the next morning. They've cleaned up the still-damp kitchen, but they can't resume work on *la obra* until a delivery truck brings more materials. The brief gap in the construction schedule coincides perfectly with Rick's plan to visit Ellen. He feels bad about the lie, but he's too embarrassed to tell the Romeros about her or about the invitation from her family.

He leaves the courtyard. Then instead of heading into town, he follows a dirt path away from Callejón Hidalgo. He's known about this path since his arrival but has rarely taken it. It leads from the Romeros' neighborhood to a cobbled road that ascends the hill overlooking Santo Domingo. Somewhere up there is *la colonia americana*. The name bothered him when he first heard it, suggesting settlers huddled together in the wilderness. But then he learned that *colonia* means "development" or "subdivision," not "colony." He has never been up there, though, and he's curious about what it will be like.

Following Ellen's directions, he walks up the road past houses that seem to get bigger and more beautiful the higher he goes. They are Mexican in design but far more elegant than those in the Romeros' barrio, with stucco walls, terra cotta roofs, wrought-iron balconies, and carefully tended trees, shrubs, and flower beds. He walks under an old stone archway. The other side reveals an even fancier neighborhood—huge houses with large fenced yards. He's running late; it's already noon, and the midday sun leaves him sweating. He begins to hurry. The blocks are so long here that a single wrong turn will throw him way off schedule.

Something hits him: Where are the people? Unlike the barrio, where people are constantly out and about, visiting in the streets or running errands on foot, this place seems deserted. He can see cars parked in driveways, often locked behind decorative metal gates. But the people themselves . . . ?

Abruptly he arrives. He stops at the wrought-iron gate and stares at the house beyond. The place is enormous. Surrounded by a wall of beautifully constructed stonework, it rises from the largest, greenest lawn Rick has seen anywhere in Santa Domingo. The house has a vaguely Mexican look because of the tile roof. But otherwise it's more American in appearance: low and flat, with windows so tall and wide, they look like glass walls.

He pushes the bell set in the wall by the gate—and waits.

A man crosses the lawn. He's wearing pressed black slacks, shiny black shoes, and a white jacket that makes him look like a waiter at an upscale restaurant. Rick identifies himself and explains that he has come to visit Ellen.

"Pase usted," the man says. You may enter. He is much older than Rick, yet he addresses him with the formality reserved for

social superiors. He turns, and Rick follows him, feeling awkward yet relieved to have reached his destination.

The house is cool inside—the first air-conditioned home Rick has been in all summer—and it seems cavernous. The living room alone looks big enough to hold the Romeros' entire property. Huge sofas sprawl about, and there's artwork everywhere—paintings, sculptures, and pieces of ancient pottery. The place is as elegant and hushed as a museum.

When the servant leads Rick through a sliding door to a patio, the mood changes completely. The scene here is full of light and color and noise. Two men and a woman sit talking at a table set in the shade of a flowering jacaranda tree. Another man sits alone at a second table. Two girls splash around in a big curved swimming pool, calling to each other and laughing. Ellen perches on the edge of the pool, her feet dangling in the water. She turns as Rick steps outside.

"Rick! You made it!" she says. Smiling, she springs up and walks over. She's wearing white shorts and a white Mexican blouse embroidered with tiny multicolored flowers. She looks even prettier than Rick remembered.

"Hi." He smiles back, aware that everyone is watching him.

Ellen leads him over to the table with the three adults. "Dad, this is Rick Dresner. Rick, this is my dad, Jack Bradshaw." She gestures to a man with sandy hair and a reddish, close-cut beard, who's wearing a green Hawaiian-print shirt.

Ellen's dad reaches across the table to shake Rick's hand. "Good to meet you."

"And this is Sandy and Pete. They work with Dad, and they're visiting from California."

More greetings, more handshakes.

Sandy and Pete are dressed more conservatively. They look friendly but slightly out of place, much like the tourists who wander the *jardín*.

Rick glances toward the man at the other table. He's a large, muscular guy with black hair and a thick black mustache. He's dressed in gray slacks, white shirt, and dark blue sports jacket, and there's a walkie-talkie resting before him on the table. The man nods at Rick, but no one introduces him.

A huge splash catches everyone's attention—the two girls cannonballing into the pool.

"My sisters," Ellen tells Rick in a tone suggesting both pride and exasperation. "Jane is eight, Marie is ten." She turns and calls to the girls, "This is Rick!"

Rick waves gamely.

Jane shouts, "Hi!" Marie sweeps her hand across the surface of the pool, flinging water upward at Rick and Ellen.

"Hey! Cut it out!" Ellen shouts as she backs off.

"Try and make me!" Marie replies.

Ellen and Rick watch the horseplay for a while. In the harsh sunshine, the water flings off great flashes of light, and he has to shield his eyes from the glare. Even so, he's dying to dive in—until he realizes that in rushing from the Romeros' house, he forgot his bathing suit.

"Ready for a swim?" Ellen asks.

"Yeah. Only one small problem," he says gloomily. "I forgot my suit."

"You're kidding! Now *that* was dumb!"

"Sorry, I just spaced out."

"Too bad." She shrugs but seems disappointed.

"Really. And I'll have to be honest, this doesn't seem like the best time or place for skinny-dipping." Rick gives her a sideways look.

She laughs. "Brilliant observation. We wouldn't want to give anyone a heart attack, would we?" She glances back toward her dad. Then she adds, "Oh, well—bring your suit next time."

Rick smiles, glad to hear her mention a next time.

They sit at their own table. The shade is cool, and there's a breeze. Fragrant lavender petals sift down on them from the jacaranda tree. After life in the cramped, noisy barrio, Rick finds the patio soothing. He could do a lot worse than to relax in this beautiful backyard.

"So what are you doing here, anyway?" Ellen asks.

"Sitting here with you," Rick tells her, "and really enjoying it."

She ignores his comment. "No, I mean in Santo Domingo."

"Living with some family friends."

"In town?"

"Sort of."

"I've seen some incredible houses down there. We know some people who own a house near the park, and they told us it's three hundred years old. They're practically living in a museum."

"That's not where my friends live," Rick says.

"Do you know them from Denver?"

"No, from here. We met when I was a kid."

She looks puzzled. "I didn't think Americans lived here till recently."

"They're not American."

Rick is aware that he's hedging. He isn't sure he wants to go into the details of his arrangement with the Romeros, so he's relieved that lunch arrives. It's the man in the black and white uniform who brings it. Wheeling a little cart, he serves the three adults first. Then he approaches Ellen's side of the table, sets a covered plate before her, and comes around to do the same for Rick—just like at a fancy restaurant. Rick notices that the man never looks directly at him or Ellen. He removes the polished steel plate covers and places them on the serving cart. Marie and Jane climb out of the pool, dry off, and sit at their own table. The servant places dishes before them and before the other man; then he leaves quietly.

There's a hamburger, some fries, and a mound of coleslaw on Rick's plate. He's pleased to see such familiar food—his first American meal in ages, it seems—and starts in eagerly. At once he's surprised by how odd it tastes, how bland after *la comida mexicana,* the Mexican food that Emiliana serves.

Ellen notices his puzzlement. "Anything wrong?"

"Not at all!" he exclaims, forcing a smile. "I was just thinking how great it is to have a good old American meal."

Looking pleased, she picks up her hamburger. "The beef's from Texas. My sisters didn't like the local stuff, so Dad ordered a hundred pounds from a company in Dallas. They shipped it down in a freezer truck."

"Wow."

"Jane and Marie won't touch Mexican food, so our cook, Guadalupe, fixes mostly American meals."

"I like Mexican food a lot."

"Me, too. Sometimes Guadalupe makes special dishes just for me. They're pretty spicy, so even my dad doesn't like them."

They eat for a while, and Rick overhears snatches of conversation from the other table.

"—partly a matter of marketing and partly the realities of software engineering."

"—and help Cybernexus achieve some sort of brand-name recognition breakthrough . . ."

"So what are *you* doing here?" he asks Ellen.

"Oh, just hanging out with my sisters. I think I mentioned . . . our parents are divorced, and we spend part of each summer with Dad. He bought this house, so here we are."

"Nice!"

"Yeah, but if you want to know the truth, I'm bored. Jane and Marie are *really* bored. They'd go nuts if they didn't have this pool."

The servant returns and asks if they'd like more food.

"You want anything?" Ellen asks. "Another hamburger?"

"I'm fine, thanks."

She shakes her head at the servant, who leaves.

"So you don't like Mexico?" Rick asks.

"Oh, I do! Especially the arts and crafts. I'm really into pottery and sculpture—I do both myself—and Mexico is such an awesome place for them. But Dad rarely lets me go anywhere alone, and he's busy all day running his software company, so I'm usually stuck here."

"Santo Domingo is pretty safe."

"That's not what Dad says."

"It's probably safer than—" Rick was going to say San Francisco, but he cuts himself short. He doesn't want to annoy Ellen. "Maybe someone else could show you around."

She misses or ignores his hint. "You mean like Sandy and Pete, the world's most exciting couple?" she asks in a low voice, gesturing to Mr. Bradshaw's visitors.

"Besides," Pete is saying, "I just don't understand how you get anything accomplished here. I can't get a reliable cell phone signal anywhere in this whole town!"

"How about your other friend?" Rick asks. He nods in the direction of the man seated near the jacaranda tree.

"That's Armando, my dad's bodyguard."

"Bodyguard!?" Rick is taken aback.

"A couple of American executives got kidnapped recently in Mexico City, so Dad arranged security protection."

"This isn't Mexico City."

Ellen looks peeved at him—not angry, just annoyed that he's not sympathizing with her plight. "Look, this is how things are," she tells him. "I don't like it, but there's not much I can do. Dad is obsessed with security. I'm lucky if I get into town once a week."

Rick decides to press the issue. "What if *I* showed you around?"

"Well—"

"I could be *your* bodyguard."

She laughs at him. "I can guard my own body, thanks."

He smiles and feels his face redden. "What I mean is—you've got nothing to be afraid of. It's a nice town. You'll like it. And I'm sure you haven't seen much of it."

"Oh, really?"

He realizes that without intending to, he has bluffed her. Most of what he knows about Santo Domingo lies within the boundaries of the Romeros' property. What is he doing, he wonders, pretending to be the great tour guide?

They talk about other things as they finish lunch. They trade stories about life back in the States. They compare notes about plans for college. Ellen tells Rick about her artwork, then shows him some projects she has underway—a mosaic of ceramic tiles near the swimming pool and, farther back in the yard, a slab of granite that she's been shaping with a mallet and chisel.

"This is cool," Rick tells her. "You're really talented."

"Thanks. I guess it helps that I'm feeling restless."

"What d'you mean?"

"Even if I weren't here, I'd be doing art," Ellen explains. "But since Dad won't let me go exploring, it's even more important for me to work on this stuff. These—projects. It makes the time go by much faster."

At these words, Rick glances at his watch—and panics. It's two twenty-five! Emiliana serves dinner at two. The Romeros will be waiting for him and surely will have held off from eating. He can't believe how long he's been away.

"I have to go," he says abruptly.

"What?"

"Sorry—I really do."

Ellen looks disappointed. "What's the rush?"

"I promised some people I'd be back earlier."

"Your Mexican friends?"

"They're almost like family."

Rick heads back toward the house. Mr. Bradshaw turns in his direction and smiles politely. "Leaving already?"

"I'm afraid so."

"Well, nice to meet you."

"Nice to meet you, too." Rick says goodbye to the others, including Armando, who nods.

Marie and Jane are back in the pool. "Hey, Ellen. Watch this!" shouts Marie. She flips forward, doing somersaults in the water, while Jane doggy paddles around her.

Rick takes in the scene: the girls splashing around, the light on the water, the breeze ruffling the jacaranda leaves—and Ellen, smiling at him, her hair shining in the afternoon sun. He's not sure he's ever seen a sight more beautiful, and he can't imagine wanting to be anywhere else in the world.

"This was great . . . wonderful . . . really fun," he says. "I'm sorry I have to go. I'll call you soon."

Ricardo Anda de Novia

"Oh, you're back," Emiliana says as Rick enters the Romeros' courtyard. She speaks without audible annoyance, but Rick feels scolded, anyway.

"Sorry I'm late."

"Are you all right?"

"I'm fine."

"*¿Quieres tu cena?*" she asks loudly. Do you want your dinner?

The truth is, he's full of the Bradshaws' Texas beef and isn't hungry. That's the least of his problems, though; he can always force down another meal. But how can he explain arriving so late?

At that moment, Francisco steps out of the living room. *"¿Qué tal?"* Rick asks in greeting.

"Bien, Ricardo," Francisco replies. He seems sort of—distant.

Fair enough, Rick thinks. After all, he's delayed everyone's meal, since the Romeros are too polite to have started without him.

Only Julio seems nonjudgmental about Rick's late arrival. "Your camera," he says when they all head into the kitchen. "Were you able to get it fixed?"

"Yes, I was," Rick replies.

Dinner is once again little more than rice, beans, and tortillas—far simpler than Emiliana's usual midday meals—but the food's simplicity does little to ease Rick's embarrassment for having showed up so late and for lying to his friends. He ignores his own mood and chatters about the afternoon's work, the weather, anything else that comes to his mind.

Julio remains relaxed about the whole situation; Francisco seems less and less concerned as the meal proceeds. But something seems to be nagging at Emiliana. She eats without looking up from her food.

Is she sick? Rick wonders. *Is she annoyed about the late dinner? Or is there some other reason she's upset?* He can't tell. He hopes she isn't feeling hurt; at the same time, he's not a bit sorry about the time he spent with Ellen. Even though he just said goodbye to her, he already misses her a lot. He wonders what she's doing . . . no doubt swimming with her sisters in the sun-bright water. Her image floats before him as the conversation continues.

"—so once it cools off this afternoon," Julio is saying, "we'll resume work on the walls we've already—"

"Do you miss your own country, Ricardo?" Emiliana asks abruptly.

Julio falls silent. Emiliana rarely interrupts her husband, and her tone of voice now is so emphatic that it catches everyone's attention.

Rick isn't sure what she's getting at, but he knows he can't evade the question. "Of course," he replies. "That's normal."

"*Déjalo, Mamacita,*" says Francisco, sounding embarrassed by his mother's interrogation. Leave him alone, Mom.

Julio offers his own comment. "Everyone has strong feelings about his country."

Emiliana won't be distracted. "But do you like it here, too?"

Rick is stunned. How could she think otherwise? For weeks on end, he has lived with the Romeros, worked with them, and shared their way of life. He's amazed that Emiliana could doubt his commitment. He says, "Of course I like it here."

"You're content with us?"

"Of course."

She seems unconvinced. She smiles at his words, but he can see some kind of sadness in her eyes. "You wouldn't prefer to be somewhere else?"

Now Francisco grows exasperated. "*¡Déjalo en paz!*" Leave him in peace!

"Believe me," Rick tells her, "I want to be here—"

"*¿Con nosotros los pobres?*" she asks. With us poor folks?

"With you because you're you. The Romeros. My friends." Rick is upset now. Because Emiliana is doubting him. Because he knows he has given her *reason* to doubt him. Because he feels that even so, he shouldn't have to explain himself like a kid justifying his behavior to a schoolteacher.

Emiliana looks calmer now, as if his words have reassured her. She reaches out and strokes his hand as it rests on the tabletop. "Forgive me, Ricardo. Forgive me. I'm sounding like a naggy old woman."

"Not at all."

"I thought you weren't happy here."

"I'm *very* happy," he tells her, grasping her hand. "Why shouldn't I be?"

Emiliana shakes her head. "Oh, I don't know. We're humble folks. We live a hard life. I thought maybe you'd gotten bored with us, or fed up."

Rick worries that she knows more than she's letting on, and he's tempted to say something that will make her drop the subject, but curiosity gets the best of him. "I don't see why you'd think that."

As if finally granted permission to speak her mind, Emiliana sits upright in her chair and gazes directly at him. Her expression isn't hostile, but it's . . . focused. "I was running errands at the marketplace this morning," she says. "On the way back, I came up El Atascadero instead of Aparicio. I saw someone who looked just like you—someone heading up toward *la colonia americana*. Nonsense, I thought. Ricardo is home with Julio."

Rick squirms in his chair. He glances at Julio and Francisco and is surprised to see them smiling at him even while Emiliana speaks.

"Once I got home, I discovered you were gone," she continues. "'Where's Ricardo?' I asked don Julio. He told me you'd gone to town to get your camera fixed. But when I saw you on El Atascadero, you weren't carrying a camera, and you were going the opposite direction. So I went to your room . . . and there was the camera on the sofa!"

Julio raises a hand. "I think we can put this discussion to rest," he says.

"He asked me, so I'm explaining," Emiliana replies. Then she turns back to Rick. "Anyway, I was worried. Then you returned home well past dinner, and you said you'd gotten your camera fixed. But I know you'd spent several hours up there in *la colonia americana*. So that is why I'm wondering if you're happy here." She sits back, folding her arms across her chest.

Rick doesn't know what to say. He has been caught, charged, tried, and found guilty. On one level, he's exasperated that the situation has turned into such a big deal. On another, he knows that his actions have offended Emiliana. Why? Because he lied? Maybe. But that isn't the whole story. Then it comes to him. Because the Romeros are so poor, all they can offer him is their hospitality. So by dashing off to hang out with gringos, he has deprived them—or Emiliana, at least—of their ability to give him this one gift. And he has made the gift seem unimportant.

"I'm sorry—" he begins. But Julio interrupts him.

"*¿No entiendes lo que ha pasado?*" Don't you know what has happened?

Who are the words intended for? Rick assumes he's the one; then he sees that Julio is speaking to his wife.

She shrugs.

"There's no mystery," Julio continues. "There's no reason to interrogate our guest like this. Ricardo is just doing what any normal boy would do, whether he's Mexican or American." He smiles warmly at Rick.

"Don't you understand?" Francisco asks his mother.

"No. I don't know what you're talking about," says Emiliana.

"Ricardo anda de novia," Julio tells her. Rick has a girlfriend.

Mulling Things Over

Rick has a girlfriend . . . *If only that were true,* he thinks as he lies in bed that night. Ellen is smart and talented and beautiful. She's friendly enough, but he doesn't really know her yet, and he's not at all sure what she thinks of him. Still, it's probably better if the Romeros believe there's a great romance taking shape, since that will help him avoid hurting their feelings. Certainly the tension at the dinner table had evaporated when he'd told them something about her. But the revelation didn't solve his biggest problem. He wants to spend more time with Ellen, and he has no idea how that can happen. Given the complex tasks involved in *la obra* and her dad's restrictions, when and where can they meet? It's not as if they can hang out at the local mall.

How odd, Rick thinks. He chose to spend the summer in Mexico partly to get away from family hassles, to gain some independence from his parents. Yet here he is, dealing with another family in almost the same ways he deals with his own. He'd hoped to find a new girlfriend, and in a sense he's succeeded— only to discover that the situation is even more complicated than if he'd started going out with someone back home. What's next? He can't even guess.

As he starts to doze off, memories of Ellen drift through his mind. He imagines kissing her, holding her, caressing her . . . But where could they find time to be alone? Rick was aware that Mr. Bradshaw stared at him during his visit, observing him closely, sizing him up. Even if Ellen wanted to spend some time at the Romeros' place, would Mr. Bradshaw let her come for a visit?

Rick sighs. There must be *some* way to deal with all these obstacles, and at least now he won't have to go sneaking around. At least now . . .

He drifts off.

Fine! Fine! Fine!

"So how are things going?" Dad asks when Rick phones home the next evening.

"Fine."

"How's the project?" Mom asks.

"Just fine."

"You're making progress, I take it?"

"Great progress." Standing in the phone booth at Teléfonos de México, Rick observes the other customers who wait to make long-distance calls. Most of them are Mexican, though some are other gringos. Rick imagines for a moment that he spots Ellen—a redhead American entering the office. Then he sees it's someone else.

"Rick," his dad is saying.

"What!"

"Are you all right?"

"Me? Fine!"

"You sound distracted."

"I thought I saw someone I know."

"Is anything the matter?" Mom asks.

He starts to feel flustered. What should he say? Yes? No? He'd like to tell his parents about Ellen and about the ins and outs of his relationship with the Romeros, and he knows his parents will be supportive. But the thought of describing all the recent events doesn't appeal to him. Too complex. Too confusing. "No, really—I'm fine," he tells them. "Everything is going just great. We're all absolutely fine."

Estoy Contenta

They continue to work on the second-story walls. The brick boxes they create—two adjacent rooms joined by a central doorway—are much bigger than Rick had anticipated. They're so empty, with vacant doorways and windows and totally bare brick walls, that his footsteps echo loudly when he walks around up there. The sky is the only ceiling.

Despite the progress on *la obra,* there's an odd mood in the Romero household—some sort of tension that Rick can't identify. Mostly what he notices is hushed conversations between Julio and Emiliana, conversations that end the moment he enters the room. The problem doesn't seem to involve him; everyone in the family is friendly. It doesn't seem to be caused by a disagreement among them; they're friendly with one another, too. What is it, then? Some sort of concern or anxiety . . . worry about Emiliana's health, perhaps? She often moves slowly, as if in pain.

Then, at supper one night—rice and beans yet again—Emiliana makes an announcement. "Ricardo, I have found employment. I have accepted a position as the cook for an American lady."

Rick isn't sure how to respond. Her face shows neither delight nor displeasure; she is simply stating a fact. Should he offer congratulations or condolences? "Will this—will it work out for you?" he asks hesitantly.

"It's very convenient. I'll be at her house each day," says Emiliana. "Then, each evening, I'll be home with my boys."

. . . *con mis muchachos.* Her words touch him. There's a wistfulness in them that makes him feel protective toward her—although he's not sure what he's protecting her from. He's also puzzled by her decision to take on a job at this particular time. Is it a promising opportunity? Or will it just be an extra load to carry?

He decides that the best thing for him to do is respond with enthusiasm. "Well—that's wonderful!" he says.

Emiliana smiles her tight-lipped smile. *"Estoy contenta."* I am content.

Accounts Payable

Entering the kitchen to get a drink of water the following afternoon, Rick finds the room empty and dim. Emiliana is off at her new job. He looks around for a glass. At some point he notices a stack of papers on the kitchen table and glances at them idly. Bills. The one on top is from the hardware company where Julio buys construction materials. The page is covered with columns of handwritten figures, the total the equivalent of seventy-five or eighty dollars. Stamped in red ink at the bottom are the words *¡Pague Inmediatamente para Evitar Cancelación de Crédito!* Pay Immediately to Avoid Cancellation of Credit!

The date on the bill is now two weeks past.

So that's why everyone is so tense, Rick thinks. *La obra* has run over budget. The Romeros are out of money. They've either borrowed to keep going, or else they're dipping into other resources—food money, perhaps?—to fill the gap. This explains why meals have been so skimpy recently. Why Francisco works part-time at SuperTienda. Why Emiliana, despite her health problems, has started a new job.

Rick is relieved to know the cause of the problem—but he has no clue how to help solve it.

A Change in the Weather

"It's time to make another *castillo*," Julio states the morning after they complete the walls.

Rick remembers this job: wiring lengths of steel rebar into elongated frameworks that rest atop the brick walls. It isn't as hard as laying brick, but it's still awkward and tedious, and lifting the completed pieces into place is tricky. All that metal weighs several hundred pounds, and being relatively flexible, it tends to flop around when moved. But the work proceeds without mishap. In two days' time, Julio and the boys assemble the *castillo* and place it along the rim of the second-story walls, with a crosspiece connecting the long walls at the middle.

As they're finishing up on the second day, after putting in almost ten hours, gray-black clouds move in from the west. In minutes, they fill the horizon and overwhelm Santo Domingo. Then the wind arrives, thrashing the trees and flinging dust and debris into the air.

"This wind wants to hurt us!" shouts Julio. While Emiliana races around the courtyard pulling down laundry from the clothesline, he and Francisco cover sacks of cement and mortar with a heavy sheet of plastic and secure the edges. Rick gathers up all the tools and puts them away. Then they all retreat to the living room.

The sun fades until it's just a dark red ball. A wall of rain moves toward Santo Domingo and devours the whole town.

Rick and the Romeros huddle together while the storm rages outside. It's too early for the evening meal, but everyone needs something to ward off the damp and chill, so Emiliana brews coffee and serves some cookies. The rain is so loud that it threatens to drown their conversation. Everyone is depressed.

"What a mess," Julio states wearily.

"Are you worried about the house?" Rick asks.

"The part we've finished? No. Once the mortar's dry, it's fine."

Francisco gazes at his father through the steam rising from his coffee cup. "What about the part that's unfinished?"

"Well, that's the problem."

"The big *colado*," Emiliana notes.

Julio nods. "Here's the thing. Once we've put up the scaffolding, we can build the upstairs bedrooms' roof. It'll be a single slab of concrete—more than double the size of the other *colado*—and we have to pour it within a single day."

"Why not in phases?" Rick asks. "Half one day, half the next?"

"That's not how a *colado* works. If some of the concrete dries and you pour a new batch next to it, the new stuff won't adhere to the old. At the very least, it could leak along the seam. It might even crack apart. So we have to put down the whole expanse at once, from one edge to the other." Julio sweeps his hand across the table.

"How much concrete, Papi?" asks Francisco.

"Four cubic meters, maybe five."

Rick flinches at the thought. Four cubic meters would weigh, what, fifteen or twenty tons? How will they ever mix that much concrete by hand?

"We'll need help," says Julio. "Alfonso and Lucho may be willing. We might invite some of the other guys in the barrio, too."

"I'm sure they'll come flocking," Emiliana says gloomily.

"They better," says Francisco. "We can't manage with just Alfonso and Lucho."

Julio raises both hands as if to hold back everyone's pessimism. "Don't worry. When the time comes—"

A sudden clatter outside makes everyone turn and stare at the door.

"*Un nahual*," whispers Julio, his eyes bulging.

Francisco groans. "Oh, *stop* it!" he says, shoving his father's shoulder.

Julio smiles. "Just kidding. It's only the storm. But that's enough to worry about. The rainy season seems to be starting early this year. If we get lots of storms like this, we're in big trouble."

"Because we won't be able to pour the *colado*?" Rick asks.

"Right. We'll have to hold off, and the rooms up there will get rained on day after day. Then, instead of bedrooms, we'll have a couple of water tanks!" He guffaws.

"Let's wait and see—and hope for the best," says Emiliana.

"We may have no other choice but to wait," Julio replies. "If we pour the concrete and then the skies open up, the rain will ruin everything we've done."

They listen to the storm for a moment. Wind hammers at the door, rattling it in its frame. A puddle starts accumulating on the floor near the entryway.

The conversation shifts to other topics—sports, food, and Francisco's upcoming interview at the teachers' college. Rick is relieved to talk about these things, but he knows what everyone is wondering: is *la obra* now doomed to fail?

Working Out

While the construction site dries out, Rick arranges to visit Ellen again. Her father has a fitness center in his house, and they spend an afternoon working out with the equipment. There's a treadmill, a stair climber, and an elliptical trainer. There's a NordicTrack and a rower. There's a full rack of free weights. Rick has never used such a well-outfitted private gym before, and it's fun to experiment without pressure. Except, of course, the pressure he feels from working out with Ellen. She's familiar with all this gear, and she's even more physically fit than he'd guessed. Wearing a green and white gym outfit, she does multiple reps with a pair of free weights. She looks strong and beautiful.

He lifts a barbell off the rack—and is startled by how much stronger he is than when he arrived in Mexico.

"You look pretty buff," Ellen says. "You must work out a lot."

"Sort of," he tells her, pleased with the compliment.

"Are there gyms in Santo Domingo?"

"I've never come across one."

"So how do you keep in shape?"

"Let's just call it on-the-job training."

Ellen sets her weights on the rack and walks over to the rower. She sits down but doesn't grab the handles. "I'd get totally out of shape if we didn't have this gym. And of course the pool. I'm used to doing lots of sports, but what I really miss is just walking places. Here, I feel like I'm under house arrest, or something. Like I'm living in a bubble. I practically never get to go places or *see* things."

Rick finishes his reps with the barbell and puts it back. The house is so thoroughly air-conditioned that he isn't even sweaty. He wanders around the gym, stretching his arms to keep them limber. "We should ask your dad if I can show you around."

"It's worth a try."

"There are lots of places we could explore."

"Sounds great."

"We could start with some of the *artesanías* workshops in the area."

"Some of the what?"

"*Artesanías.* Folk art. You can watch the people at work—weavers, silversmiths, potters, all kinds of craftspeople."

Ellen's eyes brighten. "That would be awesome. Especially seeing the potters."

"You said that pottery is something you do back home."

"Yes. I also work with stone . . . wood . . . metal."

"Cool. I'd love to watch you work."

"Well, I'd love to show you. I like making things, and I have this—I don't know—this explosive energy *that . . . wants . . . to . . . get . . . out!*" she says, her voice growing louder and louder, so that she's almost shouting by the end of her sentence.

Wandering over to the glass wall, Rick gazes out at the pool, the lawn, the hilltop, and the view of Santo Domingo beyond. The sun hangs only halfway down toward the horizon; powdery blue light hovers throughout the western sky. He checks his watch. It's four-eighteen. What's happening right now at the Romeros' house? Julio and Francisco might be working again—wiring more steel rebar to form the *castillo,* perhaps. Rick feels restless to be away from *la obra.*

"What's the matter?" Ellen asks.

"Nothing. I'm just thinking about my friends and their construction project."

"Tell me about what you're building," she says.

"It's their house. Brick walls and a concrete roof."

"You're part of the crew?"

Rick nods. "There are three of us. I'm the assistant."

"Awesome," says Ellen.

"It really is. I've learned so much."

"How do you manage all by yourselves?"

"It's hard to explain," Rick tells her. "It'd be easier just to show you."

She doesn't respond. Grabbing the rowing machine's handles, she pulls back once and lets go.

"Maybe you should come and visit." Rick speaks the words and falls silent.

"Really?"

"My friends are great people."

"I don't speak much Spanish."

"I'd translate for you."

"Well—"

"The Romeros would like you."

"Why? They'd probably just think I'm a spoiled, rich gringa," she says, looking gloomy.

"Hey, they could think *I'm* a spoiled, rich gringo," Rick tells her, "but they don't. They see me as a friend. The treat me like a family member. They like me, and they'd like you, too."

Ellen is silent for a moment. She appears to be thinking about what he's said. Then, abruptly, she says, "How about something to drink? I need a soda."

Without even glancing at Rick, she steps out of the rowing machine and leaves the room.

So much for that, Rick tells himself.

It's Not Fair

It's a couple of days later. Julio is out running an errand, Francisco has gone to the teachers' college for an interview, and Rick is tidying up the courtyard, when Emiliana comes home—six hours before she normally returns from work. Walking carefully down the patio stairs, she looks pale and exhausted, maybe even sick.

"*Buenos días, doña Emiliana,*" he calls out to her.

"*Buenos días, Ricardo.*" She heads for the kitchen, and he follows her.

"*¿Está todo bien?*" he asks. Is everything okay?

Emiliana lowers herself into a chair. "*Un poco difícil,*" she admits. A little difficult.

Rick sits down opposite her. "Your job?" he guesses.

"The *americana* dismissed me."

"Dismissed you!"

"She says I'm incompetent. She says I'm totally good-for-nothing."

"What? How can she say that?" Rick demands. "After all you've done—"

"She can say anything she wants. She's the boss."

Emiliana tells him the story. It turns out that the American woman's behavior was abusive from the start. She expected Emiliana not only to cook meals—her stated duty—but also to clean house and run errands. When Emiliana pointed out that she had been hired solely to cook, the woman threatened to fire her immediately. Emiliana stopped protesting in fear of losing her job. The situation deteriorated further. The *americana* ranted all day, both in English and in nearly incomprehensible Spanish, and she demanded constant work from Emiliana.

"'Mop the floor! Dust the shelves! Wash the windows!' she screamed at me," says Emiliana, her voice rising to a screech. "Then she'd yell, 'Where's my lunch? I asked you to fix me lunch!' Well, I was too busy cleaning, so what did she expect?"

She ordered Emiliana to run errands to a pharmacy, then threw bottles of medicine on the floor because the pharmacist had misinterpreted her scribbles and bad Spanish. Finally, she accused Emiliana of stealing some of her imported American cookies.

"I told her, 'I may be poor. I may be uneducated. But before God in heaven, I swear I'm not a thief.' She said she didn't like my tone and told me to leave the house at once."

"It's not fair," Rick says.

Emiliana glances at him but doesn't respond. She dabs at her eyes with a handkerchief.

"You shouldn't have to work under such awful conditions."

She sighs. "Unfortunately, that's just how it is."

Rick is furious about the way *la americana* has treated Emiliana. He'd like nothing better than to go over to the woman's house and yell at her, really tell her what an idiot she is. But he knows this isn't likely to help. In fact, it might make everything much worse. *La americana* is an adult—by all accounts a troubled, unstable adult, but still . . . She wouldn't tolerate being scolded by a teenager, and she might make big trouble for Emiliana. So what's to be done?

"Maybe we'll find you another job," Rick tells her. "Something better."

Emiliana nods without much enthusiasm. "There's so little work."

"I'll ask around. I'm sure we can find something."

"I hope so," she says, "but it's going to be difficult. Usually it's younger people, stronger people, who get the jobs. Not many will hire an old woman like me."

It makes Rick sad to hear Emiliana speak of herself as old, yet right now, as tired and discouraged as she is, she *looks* old. "There's got to be *someone* who will appreciate what you have to offer," he says, patting her hand.

She sits up straighter now, as if rousing herself. "Please pardon me for saying what I'm about to say," Emiliana tells him. "That woman is crazy, but even sane employers have treated me poorly. They make me work all day and allow me almost no time to rest. They have me fix huge, fancy meals for them, but they provide only a bit of food for me. Ten, twelve hours a day I work. When it's almost time to go, they say, 'Can't you stay awhile longer? Here are a few more clothes I'd like you to wash. And before you go, please scrub the sinks, tub, and toilets.' No, I'm afraid it's not quite so easy to find a good employer."

"What about working for Mexicans?"

"It's generally the same. Please understand me—it's not a question of nationality but of wealth. Whether American or Mexican, the rich treat us pretty much the same. They treat us like dogs."

Rick feels something inside him shift abruptly. "This is crazy!" he exclaims, pushing back his chair and standing.

Emiliana looks both startled and amused.

Before she can respond, Rick goes on. "The money isn't worth the trouble. When I said it isn't fair, I meant it. When I said you shouldn't have to work under these conditions, I meant that, too. No one should."

"What's to be done?" she asks, gesturing uncertainly.

"Well—maybe nothing. I mean, nothing about that obnoxious *americana*. I can't make her treat you better, can I? But I can help you get away from her—and all these other people, too." He sits back down, pleased with himself. He has an answer. He'll loan them the money to finish *la obra*. No, he'll *give* them the money.

Emiliana still looks confused. "What are you telling me?"

"I don't think you should work for someone like that."

"As I said—"

"Or anyone else."

"But I need to work so we can to afford—" At once an expression of dismay and embarrassment comes over Emiliana's face. He sees that she's starting to understand. "*Ay*, Ricardo. You mustn't."

"I'm here to help, so let me help."

She looks trapped. "That isn't why I told you all this."

"I know. But I can't just stand by while that woman abuses

you. If there's no good work available, then don't even bother! We'll solve the problem ourselves." Rick feels a growing sense of pride as he grasps how easily he can make a difference to the Romeros. "I'll contribute whatever you need for your finances. Whatever is necessary to finish *la obra*."

Emiliana looks horrified. "What will your parents think?"

"They'll back me up. They'll be just as angry as I am about how you've been treated." Watching her react to what he's saying, Rick feels surprised to see the dismay and discomfort in her expressions. This wasn't what he expected. Why isn't she pleased?

Emiliana won't meet his gaze. "It wouldn't be fair to them," she says.

"They'll insist. You know how much they care about you."

He can see her eyes welling up. "It just doesn't seem right."

"*I* insist, too."

For a while they sit there silently. Rick wants to say something but holds off. He's aware that this conversation hasn't gone as he'd expected, but he's not sure exactly why or how to make things right again. He keeps hoping that Emiliana will somehow reassure him.

"*Gracias, Ricardo,*" she says at last.

There's no alternative now but to finish what he started. He stops by his room to pick up his wallet, says a quick goodbye to Emiliana, and heads for town. The steep Callejón Catarata is the quickest way down, so he takes that route. Within eight or ten minutes, he's at the bank. After entering the ATM booth, he accesses the account his parents set up for travel emergencies, makes a debit card withdrawal for the equivalent of two hundred dollars, and leaves with an envelope full of pesos in his pocket.

These are his friends, Rick tells himself as he heads back up the hill. He can't solve *all* their difficulties. But he can at least keep Emiliana out of the clutches of people like the crazy *americana*.

"Here's what we discussed," he tells Emiliana on returning. He holds out the envelope.

She stares at it a moment, then takes it. "Thank you," she says. She doesn't open it. She just stands there. "I guess I'd better put this somewhere safe," she finally says. Then she turns and walks out of the kitchen.

Rick heaves a deep sigh, wondering if he should have handled things differently. Should he have put the money in the bedroom, so Emiliana could find it instead of having to take it from him? Should he have given it to Julio instead? His uneasiness is all too familiar. He knows that his intentions are good, but he also sees that he has somehow hurt his friend's pride.

Dismayed, he leaves the room, crosses the courtyard, and climbs the few steps into the living room. He sits on the sofa.

Soon after that, Emiliana appears in the doorway. *"Perdóname."* Excuse me.

Rick stands. "Please come in."

She enters, taking what appear to be uncomfortable steps. After hesitating a moment, she opens her arms and embraces Rick. "Thank you," she says.

He hugs her back. He can tell that she's weeping.

Emiliana gently disengages. "It's not just the money I appreciate. It's what you said about the job. That it isn't fair. That I shouldn't have to work under such conditions."

Rick gestures awkwardly. "Well, I meant it."

"Thank you."

"It's okay."

She smiles her prim smile, but she looks exhausted. "Now I'm going to rest."

Feeling relieved, Rick watches her walk out of the room.

Negotiations

"Things are a bit . . . difficult here," Rick tells his parents when he speaks with them by phone that evening.

"How so?" his father asks. "Do you mean the construction isn't going well, or your relationship with the Romeros is a problem, or what?"

"Things are tight. They're financially difficult."

"What's going on?" his mother asks.

Rick can feel his skin prickle with annoyance. The phone connection is so good that his parents might well be a block away. He can even hear them inhaling and exhaling. "What's going on," he says slowly, "is what usually goes on when things get tight. We ran out of money."

"Look," Dad says, "we're not trying to interrogate you."

"I know that."

"You sound a bit snappy."

"Sorry."

"We're just not sure we understand the situation," Mom says.

"I'm not sure I do, either," Rick confesses. "Maybe Julio underestimated the cost of materials. Maybe the prices went up. Anyway, we've spent all of their savings."

"That's what Julio said?" Dad asks.

"No, I just figured it out. Francisco's working part time. Emiliana took a job, too, but then her crazy boss fired her a few days later."

"Poor Emiliana."

"She was crushed, believe me, because they're really short on cash. I saw some of their bills, and they're behind in payments for construction materials. They've even cut back on food."

"And now you're in a bind," Dad says.

"That's about the size of it. So to help them out, I took two hundred bucks from the ATM."

A long silence follows, and Rick wonders if he has somehow lost the connection. "Dad? Mom?"

"We're here," Mom says.

"Just doing some calculations," Dad says.

Rick is pretty sure his parents don't have much cash to spare. College is just a year away, and they haven't figured out yet how to cover all the costs. "Look," he tells them, "I'll get a part-time job this fall to make it up. At the library. The supermarket. Whatever it takes." He feels more and more agitated as he speaks.

"Hang on a sec," Mom says.

"Really. I'll find something." He's thinking fast. "I can mow lawns or rake leaves or something."

"Rick—"

"I don't care what it is, if I can help get the Romeros out of a bind."

Mom cuts in before he can go on. "I can tell this is important, Rick. To Julio and Emiliana and Francisco—and to you," she says. "That means it's important to us, too. You should know that. We'll find a way to cover the added expense."

"Well—thanks." Rick exhales suddenly, unaware that he'd been holding his breath. "That's great. Thanks again."

La Panza Blanca

"*¿Qué tal la panza blanca?*" Julio asks Rick with a smile.

Rick can't make sense of the question. Maybe it's too early for his brain to function. It's barely seven in the morning, after all, and everyone has just sat down to breakfast. Or maybe its Julio's words that are the problem. *Qué tal* Rick understands: "How is." Then *panza* means "belly," and *blanca* means "white." So far so good, but the words still don't add up. "How's the white belly?"

Francisco shakes his head at his father. "Papi . . ."

Emiliana, setting down plates of *huevos rancheros* and tortillas, is far more blunt in her warning. "*No molestes a Ricardo con tus porquerías de mojado.*" Don't pester Rick with your wetback nonsense.

Julio ignores her, intent on pursuing whatever is on his mind. "Let me explain," he says. "Out in the high desert, you'll find two kinds of rabbits. *Pardos* are the brown ones. *Panzas blancas* are light-colored." He smiles in amusement.

"Guess where this is going," Francisco says, nudging Rick.

Rick nods knowingly. "I get it," he says.

Julio continues as if he hadn't been interrupted. "So we guys have nicknames for women. Mexicans are *pardas,* and Americans are *panzas blancas.*"

"*Ay, don Julio,*" mutters Emiliana, rolling her eyes. She fixes a plate for herself, then sits down to eat.

Rick decides to ignore the slang and answer the question. "Ellen is fine."

"She's happy here in Santo Domingo?" asks Julio.

"I guess so." Rick doesn't want to go into details.

Emiliana continues the questioning. "Is she a student?"

"Well, yes—back in the States. Right now she's on summer vacation, like me."

"Her family lives up there in *la colonia americana?*"

"Just Ellen, her dad, and her sisters. Her mom lives somewhere else."

"Ah," says Emiliana. "Divorced?"

"Yes."

"The girl must be lonely."

Francisco seems increasingly impatient with his mother's interest in Ellen, but it's Julio who interrupts. *"Pues, ¡invítale a la panza blanca que nos visite!"* Well, invite the "white belly" to visit us!

Rick grins. A visit from Ellen is just what he's been hoping for. It would be great to be with her *and* the Romeros.

"Good idea," says Emiliana. "We'd love to have her as our guest."

Francisco nods without smiling.

"She can experience the real Mexico," Julio adds, spreading his arms wide as if to encompass the entire barrio.

Oh, yeah, Rick thinks, *the* real *Mexico.* At once he has second thoughts about this plan. What would Ellen think of the neighborhood and of the Romeros? And what, for that matter, would they think of *her?*

The Three Rs

Sitting in the shade of the *pirul* during siesta time that afternoon, Rick writes postcards to his friends back home. He realizes at some point that Hilaria is watching him from the kitchen doorway. *"Vente,"* he says with a smile, and beckons to her.

She comes and sits beside him. She doesn't say much; she seems content to just keep him company. After a while, he turns back to his postcard—a quick message to Jason—and resumes scribbling.

"How do you write so fast?" Hilaria asks suddenly, almost shouting in amazement.

Her comment surprises him. He isn't writing all *that* fast. "I don't know . . . That's just how I write," he replies.

"You're really good!"

"Well, it comes with practice," he tells her. "I'm sure you'll write fast, too, some day."

A shadow comes over her expression. "No, I won't," she says.

"Sure you will."

"I don't think so."

"They'll teach you in school."

"No, they won't."

"Sure they will—along with reading and arithmetic, right?"

Hilaria doesn't answer. Although she's still right next to him, she has withdrawn so far into herself that she may as well be a hundred miles away. Her smile is gone, and she won't meet Rick's gaze.

It's a hot day, but a chill comes over him. "You *do* go to school, don't you?" he asks.

"No," she replies in a flat tone.

"No? Why not?"

"My parents won't let me."

Rick is appalled. He wants to shout, *Won't let you? What kind of parents won't let their kid go to school?* But he doesn't want to upset her even more. Instead, he asks, "Oh? And why is that?"

"So I can earn money from Auntie," says Hilaria, "and then Mami and Papi can buy some extra food."

Now he understands. Emiliana and Julio have almost no money, but as little as they have, they're doing what they can to help Hilaria and her family.

Rick and Hilaria sit for a while without talking, the silence heavy between them. He's relieved when she somehow returns from her state of exile, reaches over, and takes the ballpoint pen from his hand. She clicks it over and over. The point pokes out of the shaft, then retracts; pokes out, then retracts. She snickers. "It's like a snake sticking out its skinny little tongue!" she exclaims.

"Would you like the pen?" Rick asks.

She looks stunned. She reaches out quickly to give it back.

"No—keep it. It's for you, Hilaria."

"*¿De veras?*" Really?

"*De veras.*"

She starts clicking it again—the snake's tongue poking out, then retracting, over and over.

"And I'll tell you what," Rick says suddenly. "I'll teach you how to write your name."

She turns to him and smiles that perfect smile of hers. "*¿De veras?*"

"*De veras.*"

Departures

"Juan, Alfonso, and Lucho leave for Texas tomorrow," Julio states as they sit down to the evening meal.

Francisco nods once, then helps himself to a toasted *bolillo*. He seems to have expected this news.

Emiliana is standing at the burners, filling bowls with lentil soup. "Well," she says without turning, "may God protect them."

Rick isn't sure if he should step into this family discussion, but finally he asks, "Do you think we could talk them out of it?"

"I'm not sure it's worth trying," says Julio.

"Alfonso and Lucho will do whatever helps their mother," says Emiliana, setting bowls before Rick, Francisco, and Julio, "and right now that probably means traveling *al norte*. As for their father, only God knows why that man does what he does. How can he walk for days in the desert when he can't even walk a straight line? But you can't reason with him. He'd try walking to the moon if he thought he could find a few pesos for booze up there." She serves herself and sits down.

"Isn't it an awfully big gamble?" Rick asks.

"Of course," says Emiliana. "But it's a gamble if Alfonso and Lucho stay here, too. What's their mother to feed the little ones? What's she supposed to do if her husband is a drunkard and her oldest son doesn't try to earn a living wage?"

Rick shrugs, knowing there's no answer. The sadness in the room weighs on him—weighs on all of them.

Emiliana stirs her soup absent-mindedly. "Don't get me wrong. Alfonso and Lucho are good sons. They'll do what's right for their family. They know that going *al norte* is dangerous, but they'll do it, or anything else, if it helps the family survive. Unfortunately, there aren't any good alternatives."

"Maybe they'll be okay," Francisco says.

"Let's hope God takes pity on them," adds Emiliana.

Julio and the boys eat for a while. Rick is relieved when Emiliana finally starts to eat, too.

Then Julio says, "I'm sorry to see Alfonso and Lucho go, but not just for their sake." He nods upward.

At first Rick doesn't understand. Is this a religious gesture? Is he begging for divine mercy? Then he gets it. Julio is simply motioning toward the ceiling—not the ceiling right overhead, but the one that doesn't exist yet. "The *colado*?" he asks.

Julio nods. "They were going to help us. We really need them to do the job."

"Ay," mutters Emiliana.

There's no conversation for a while; the only sounds are the clicking of spoons on ceramic bowls. Then Francisco asks, "So . . . what are we going to do?"

"I don't know," says Julio. "We'll have to see who else is dumb enough to help us."

Serenading the Neighborhood

A few days later, on returning from an errand to the hardware store—and a quick call to Ellen—Rick encounters Rodolfo. He's sitting on a wall that juts out from his family's house, strumming his guitar, and singing. *"No me hagas sufrir, morenita de mis sueños,"* he croons in his smooth tenor voice. Don't make me suffer, brunette of my dreams.

"Isn't it a bit early for a serenade?" Rick teases.

"What do gringos know about serenades!" exclaims Rodolfo in mock outrage. "Only latinos understand."

"Hah! Even a gringo can see it's eleven twenty in the morning," Rick shoots back. "Where's the romantic moonlight?"

"Who needs moonlight!"

"Where's the lovely señorita?"

Rodolfo strums a dissonant chord. *"Vete, gringo."* Get lost, gringo.

"Just joking," Rick says. Then he changes the subject. "Any word from your dad and brothers?"

"Not yet."

"I hope they're okay."

"God will protect them."

"How's the rest of your family?"

Strumming a few chords, Rodolfo shrugs. "Sometimes fine, sometimes not."

Rick doesn't want to intrude further, but he's concerned about Rodolfo's family—especially Hilaria, his favorite. "I know times are tough," he says.

"There's no work."

Rick wonders if he should talk to Rodolfo about *la obra*. Maybe Julio has already done so . . . or maybe not, given what happened last time. But he decides to go ahead, anyway. "We have a big job coming up—another *colado*," he says.

"So I hear."

"You should talk to don Julio."

"Uncle is angry at me," Rodolfo states gloomily. "He thinks I'm a lazy bum."

"If you just talk to him, I think he'll be open-minded."

"I didn't do a damn thing last time."

"Well, there's always next time."

"You think so?" Rodolfo sings the words, the last syllable a syrupy vibrato.

"He needs you. You need him," Rick says. "Talk to him."

The only answer is a chord sequence as Rodolfo starts to sing his next song.

Arts and Crafts

Out on the town, with Mr. Bradshaw's approval, Rick and Ellen visit a folk art cooperative. Santo Domingo is already well known as a place for tourists to buy Mexican *artesanías*. Many shops and galleries sell pottery, metalwork, jewelry, textiles, and other goods from every region in the country. Now a couple of enterprising Mexican businessmen have taken the idea one step further, setting up a site where people can watch regional artisans at work. There are coppersmiths from Santa Clara del Cobre, silversmiths from Taxco, weavers from Oaxaca and Michoacán, potters from Puebla, Tonalá, and Tlaquepaque . . .

"This is so cool!" Ellen exclaims as they enter the renovated warehouse. Each artisan has a separate work area in the subdivided space. There's a fair amount of noise, but it's not unpleasant. Hammering, mostly. A few radios playing Mexican music. The murmur of conversation. They've arrived early, and the place is almost empty of tourists.

Wandering with Ellen among the workshops, Rick puts his arm around her waist and is delighted when she responds the same way. He's happy to be with her, happy that they're exploring this place together.

First they watch a jeweler embedding turquoise in a silver bracelet. Then they shift their attention to a pair of coppersmiths who pull a fat slab of copper from the furnace and pound it with their big hammers to make a large kettle.

Ellen is grinning widely, clearly excited by all the sights and sounds. "What I'd really like to see," she says, "are the potters."

"Let's find them."

Within a few minutes they've discovered the pottery workshop. Two men wearing jeans, white T-shirts, and Mexican cowboy hats sit behind huge potters' wheels. One of them is preparing his wheel. The other is already at work, manipulating the mass of clay in his hands to form an *olla,* a cooking pot.

"Buenos días," Rick says.

"Muy buenos días," answers the first potter.

The one who's working glances their way and smiles.

"He makes it look so easy," Ellen tells Rick. She watches for a while in silence, totally focused on the pot taking shape.

Rick in turn watches Ellen, amazed by how different she looks, how happy and relaxed, now that something has captured her attention.

"You think they'd let me take a turn?" she asks suddenly. "Just for a few minutes?"

Rick gestures uncertainly. "I'm afraid they'll feel put on the spot."

"Will you ask them? Please?" She bounces on her toes with excitement, reminding Rick of Hilaria. "They'll say yes or no, won't they? Simple as that. Pretty please, Rick?"

The one potter still hasn't started work. Hesitantly, Rick explains Ellen's request. *"Unos pocos minutos, nada más,"* he adds. Just a few minutes.

"Perdóname, pero no se puede." Sorry, but it can't be done. He looks embarrassed by having to refuse this pretty gringa.

Ellen clasps her hands before her. "Please?" she asks, smiling beseechingly. *"¿Por favor?"*

The potters exchange glances and speak to each other in Spanish that's too fast for Rick to follow. Then the one beckons Ellen to enter the work area.

"Oh, thank you! *¡Gracias!*" She comes around quickly, takes a seat at the potter's wheel, and sets to work.

Rick isn't sure what to expect, but right away he's impressed. It's not just what Ellen is doing: coaxing the clay into shape on the wheel. It's also Ellen herself—her calm, her focus, her physical strength, and her control over the equipment. He's witnessing a side of her that he has suspected exists but that he hasn't seen until now, a side that isn't bored or impatient. She looks confident, powerful, and totally involved in what she's doing.

The potters, too, are impressed. One of them whistles through his teeth. The other says, *"¡Ay!"* flinching as if from a half-pleasant pain.

She works for a while, easing her hands into the clay, shaping it until a graceful pot emerges. She seems transfixed by the effort, unaware of the people watching her. Then, abruptly, she slows the wheel and shoves the pot back into itself until it's just a gray heap on the wheel. She gets up from the bench.

"¡Gracias, gracias!" she says to the potters. She washes her hands at a nearby sink; then she and Rick say goodbye and walk on. He notices that more tourists have entered the warehouse now—middle-aged couples, parents with kids, and gray-haired seniors. Some of them scarcely look around before they pull out their cameras and start snapping photos.

Ellen is still buzzing from her experience at the potter's wheel. "That was awesome! I could've done that all day!" she exclaims.

"Those guys probably would have let you," Rick says.

"It felt so great to be working again."

"I could tell."

She looks perplexed. "Really? How?"

"I've never seen you look so happy."

"Well, I was."

"You look totally different when you're actually *doing* something."

"Meaning . . . what?"

"Well, you're an artist. You have creative energy, right? You want to roll up your sleeves and get your hands dirty, not just stand around and gawk and take pictures." He gestures at the tourists.

She looks flattered by his words but somehow annoyed, too. "Great. So what am I supposed to do?"

"*Make* something."

"Like what!"

"Throw pots at home."

"I don't have a studio."

"Build them some other way."

"I don't have the equipment or materials."

Rick loses patience. "Isn't part of being an artist figuring things out? What to make and how to make it?"

"Of course, but—"

"So what are you waiting for?"

"That's easy for *you* to say," Ellen tells him, raising her voice. "You have your big fat project to keep you busy. I have nothing." She turns toward him. "Listen—I don't even want to be here!

Mexico is wonderful, don't get me wrong, but I'd much rather be in California, where I've got my studio and the freedom to actually *do* stuff. The only reason I'm here is because of my parents' stupid custody arrangement."

"Ellen—"

"I'm old enough to decide which parent I want to live with, right? But I live with my mom most of the year, so my dad will be pissed if I refuse to spend the summer with him. And my sisters are supposed to have these months with him, and they like to be with me, so *they'll* be pissed if I don't come along, too."

Rick feels terrible. He had no intention of upsetting her like this.

"So here's the situation," she says, close to tears now. "I'm not trying to be negative. If I was back home and working in my studio, I could be really, really positive. But being here, I'm just kind of . . . *stuck*." She falls silent and stares at him, with those intense, almost fierce, green eyes.

Rick reaches out a hand. "Ellen, I'm really sorry. I didn't mean . . ."

For a moment, she can't seem to speak. "Never mind. Forget it," she says at last. "Let's just look at more of the workshops, okay?"

She takes his hand and they move on.

Work and Work and Work

A new load of *vigas* and *cimbra* arrives, more than double the quantity Julio had rented last time, since the *colado* they'll lay now will be over twice the size of the first one. He and Francisco and Rick spend all morning carrying the beams and boards from the drop-off spot to the house, then stack everything in the second-floor rooms. It's a much more difficult task than before, not just because of the increased quantity of materials but also because of the conditions. A light rain spatters them, and blustery winds whirl through the *callejón,* shoving them sideways as they carry the awkward loads. They're finished in time for the midday meal, however, and collapse into their seats as Emiliana serves dinner.

Rick is almost too tired to eat, but the aroma of her cooking inspires him. He takes a few bites of enchilada, then starts gobbling.

The Romeros chuckle at the sight. "This'll put some meat on your bones," Emiliana tells him, reaching out to squeeze his left bicep. "We'll fatten you up for Mama!"

"Eat hearty," says Julio. "You'll need energy for this afternoon."

"We're going to keep working?" asks Francisco, sounding shocked.

"What choice have we got?"

"I thought we'd let up for today."

Rick had assumed the same thing—that they'd stop work, or at least slow down, as they often do following particularly tough tasks. He's so tired, he's dizzy. But what really concerns him is a plan he'd worked out with Ellen for a brief afternoon visit at her dad's house.

Julio pushes pieces of enchilada onto his fork with a rolled tortilla. "I wish we could rest. I'm tired, too. But we can't risk it—*la obra* is running late."

"It's raining," says Emiliana.

"Not very hard. It's sprinkling, that's all. We can put up beams in this weather, so we have to grab the chance. Otherwise, at some point we may find ourselves waiting and waiting to do the *colado*, but the opportunity will have passed."

"All right, let's get back to work," Francisco mutters.

"Rick should rest," Emiliana states firmly.

"Fine," says Julio.

Rick is far from eager to keep working, but he also resents being coddled. "I won't rest."

"You're exhausted," Emiliana protests.

"So are they," Rick says, gesturing to the others. "If *they* work, I work."

Julio raises a hand to object. "Ricardo, the two of us can manage."

"I really want to help."

Smiling, Julio shrugs. *"Como quieras."* As you wish.

Rick takes only enough time off to race down Callejón Hidalgo to the *bodega*. If he can't see Ellen, he wants at least to explain why.

"Hello?" she says when he reaches her from the pay phone.

"It's Rick."

"Hi! Are you coming?" She sounds friendly, eager.

He was already hungry to be with her, and now he feels all the more so. "Sorry, I can't," he says. "Something's come up with the construction project."

"Oh."

He feels his mood sinking. He can tell she's disappointed, too. "Ellen, I'm sorry. Until about ten minutes ago, I thought I'd make it. Then my friends decided to keep working till dusk."

There's a brief silence. "Well, do what you have to."

"I hope you understand."

"Of course."

"We can't lose our momentum on the project."

"Right."

"How about tomorrow?" he suggests, trying to sound upbeat. "We could—"

"Tomorrow isn't good. Dad is taking us along on a visit to some business people in a town called Queré— Queré—"

"Querétaro."

"Whatever-o. Nobody wants to go, but Dad insists."

"How about if I call you in the evening?"

"Great."

"Talk to you then."

Rick knows he's letting her down. Yet if he'd gone up the hill to visit her, he would've let the Romeros down. He can't win. What makes matters worse is Julio's annoyingly cheerful question on his return: "*¿Qué tal tu novia?*" How's your girlfriend?

Help Wanted

Soon the upper rooms will be ready for their new roof. "We really ought to have six men for the *colado*," Julio explains at the supper table. "Two guys to mix batches of concrete in the patio. Two guys to carry the buckets up to the roof. And two guys to lay the concrete. It has to go like clockwork." He strikes his left palm with his right hand. "Bam, bam, bam! Otherwise we can't pull it off."

"Can't we get by with fewer people?" Rick asks. "Maybe Francisco and I could mix the concrete, then haul it up to you."

Julio shakes his head. "It has to be a continuous process: mixing, hauling, and laying concrete simultaneously."

"It's hard work. Real hard—*you* know that from the first *colado*," adds Francisco. "Without the right number of people, the process will break down, and everyone will get too exhausted to keep going."

"Francisco and I can lay the concrete. Ricardo can either mix or carry," says Julio. "We need three other guys."

"Alfonso and Lucho are in Texas, so they're out of the picture," says Emiliana. "But *I* can help carry."

There's a respectful silence before Julio says, "It's out of the question. Your back problems are bad enough already."

No one argues—not even Emiliana.

"What about Rodolfo?" asks Rick.

Another silence, different from the first. "He can provide background music," Francisco says at last.

Everyone laughs.

"I *did* mention the job to him," Rick says, "and it *seemed* like he was interested in working."

"Well, *that's* a first," says Emiliana with a snort of amusement.

"Can't we give him a chance?"

"Too risky," says Julio. "He's unreliable."

"There must be other guys in the neighborhood," says Francisco.

Emiliana nods. "Arturo Sánchez and his brother, what's his name?"

"Aurelio."

"Right, Aurelio."

"They're good," Julio states, "but they're off picking strawberries in California."

"Jorge Chávez?"

"He's got a new job in Celaya."

"Chuy Moro?"

"Not a safe bet. He'd be willing, but he's got a bad knee that acts up a lot."

They run through as many names as they can recall. Scribbling on a scrap of paper, Francisco notes the few that he and his parents consider promising. They all look discouraged about this situation.

"I'm sure we can find someone," Rick says, trying to dispel the gloom.

"Maybe so," Julio responds, "but it won't be easy. Everyone has to work as a team. And very few people will tolerate such exhausting work."

Rick nods at these last words but doesn't add what he's

thinking. He already feels as if he's running on fumes. Can *he* tolerate any more of this exhausting work?

First Aid

The next morning, shortly after breakfast, Remedios appears at the Romeros' house. She speaks briefly to Emiliana, who then turns to Rick. *"Tienes una curita?"* she asks him. Do you have a Band-Aid?

"I have a first-aid kit in my room," he answers. "Do you have a cut, Remedios?"

"No—Hilaria does."

"Hang on. I'll be back in a moment."

He gets his kit and returns to the courtyard. "Here you are," he says, handing Remedios several Band-Aids.

She smiles in embarrassment. "These are too small."

Rick feels a twinge of alarm. "How big is the cut?"

"Bigger than this," replies Remedios, holding her thumb and forefinger a couple of inches apart.

"You're kidding," he says, shocked.

"She fell and hit her head."

Within minutes, Emiliana and Rick are at the house next door. Julio is off doing an errand, but Francisco comes with them. It's so dark inside that Rick can't tell at first who's there. Once his eyes adjust, he sees the two youngest children huddled together, both of them weeping, on a bed. Rodolfo is at a tiny table, eating breakfast. Antonia sits near the only window, holding Hilaria in her lap.

"¿Qué pasó, sobrina?" Emiliana asks gently. What happened, niece?

Both mother and child are too upset to speak. Antonia simply rocks her daughter back and forth. Hilaria stares, wide-eyed, at the visitors.

"She fell off the ladder in back," states Rodolfo calmly, scooping up beans with a tortilla. "She cut her head on a rock when she hit the ground."

Stepping around to see Hilaria in the light, Rick can tell at once that the situation is far worse than he expected. There's a gash nearly two inches long in the girl's forehead. Puffy and red, it looks like an open mouth. Blood drools down her face. It's such a gruesome sight that Rick immediately feels sick to his stomach. "She needs a doctor!" he exclaims.

"She'll be fine," announces Rodolfo.

"Ay, Santa María, have pity on us!" wails Antonia in a shrill voice.

"I cleaned the cut," says Rodolfo.

Rick realizes that among the odors in the room is something rank and oily. "What did you use?" he asks, trying to keep his voice calm.

"Kerosene."

"Kerosene!"

"It kills the germs."

Rick's alarm keeps growing. Kerosene—on a bad cut! "Is there a hospital in town?" he asks.

"No, but there's an emergency clinic," says Francisco.

"Let's get her there."

"Forget it!" shouts Rodolfo, standing and shoving back his chair. "I said she's fine!"

Rick gestures in frustration. "She really needs to go—"

"Keep out of this, gringo!"

"I'm just trying to help."

"Take your help back *al norte.*"

Rick cocks his fist, but before he can swing a punch, Emiliana grabs his arm. "Listen to me," she tells her nephew. "What do *you* know about what your sister needs?"

"I know we can't afford that fancy clinic!" Rodolfo shouts.

"Hilaria is hurt."

"She should have been more careful."

"Careful?" Emiliana exclaims. "How can she be careful when your lazy father didn't even put in a proper staircase up to the second floor?"

"Don't insult my father!"

The children are crying louder now, frightened by all the shouting. Only Hilaria remains silent. Rick wonders if she's going into shock.

"I'll insult your father all I want," says Emiliana. "God knows, the man deserves every insult I can come up with."

Francisco interrupts. "Let's not argue anymore. We have to get Hilaria to the clinic."

"We don't have the money!" screams Rodolfo, slapping the tabletop.

Emiliana and Francisco exchange a tense glance.

Rick knows that the Romeros don't have the money, either. *"Yo mismo lo pago,"* he blurts out. I'll pay for it myself.

Everyone stares at him.

Rick doesn't know what else to say. He has no idea what the clinic will cost. All he knows is that Hilaria has suffered a serious blow to the head, she's badly cut, and she needs medical care. How can he ignore the situation?

"Let's just get her to the clinic," he says.

Rick fastens some big Band-Aids to Hilaria's forehead, Francisco picks her up, and the three of them, along with Emiliana, Antonia, and Rodolfo, head down the hillside to *el centro*. Remedios stays behind with the two little ones.

When they reach the clinic, a doctor and nurse size up Hilaria's injury and determine that there's no fracture or concussion. It's a simple laceration. They'll clean, anesthetize, and suture the wound.

Hilaria cooperates with her usual silent acceptance—until she sees the needle for the anesthetic, at which point she panics, screaming loudly. She quiets down only when the doctor agrees to allow not just her mother, but Rick as well, into the procedure room.

Rick feels faint as he watches the doctor stitch Hilaria's forehead. But he forces himself to stay calm for her sake, to concentrate on the small hand placed so trustingly in his larger one. Once the nurse applies a gauze pad and some tape, the ordeal is over.

The bill for all this medical care, it turns out, is the equivalent of about eighteen dollars. Rick pays without hesitation, amazed that the cost is so low and glad to ease the burden on Hilaria's family. Antonia and Emiliana thank him several times.

Walking back to the barrio, Rick is struck by the silence. No one speaks. Hilaria has good reason; she's exhausted by her trauma. Antonia must be tired, too. But Emiliana and Francisco also say nothing, and Rodolfo stalks ahead of the group, keeping far away from Rick.

"Is everything okay?" he asks Francisco once they're back at the house.

"*Completamente,*" is the answer. "*Gracias a Dios.*"

"*Pobrecita,*" says Rick. Poor little girl.

"Everything worked out all right," says Francisco in a flat tone. Then he heads upstairs and starts getting organized for the day's work.

Baffled, Rick retreats to the kitchen for a glass of water, which lets him encounter Emiliana as if by accident. "Why is everyone so tense?" he asks.

"Tense?"

"Rodolfo's angry. Okay, I understand that. We had an argument. But no one else is talking much either."

"Everyone's just exhausted, Ricardo," she assures him. "We were all terribly worried about Hilaria."

"Of course," he replies, but he knows that this isn't the whole story.

Emiliana turns away and goes about her business, pouring dried beans into a pan to rinse and soak. "Everything's fine," she says.

Rick stares at her back. This all feels too familiar. He decides to press the point. "What am I supposed to do, Emiliana?" he says quietly. "I know it makes people . . . uncomfortable . . . when I pay for something. But I have the money. So wouldn't it be worse if I *didn't* pay? Wouldn't that offend people more?"

"You haven't offended anyone."

"It sure seems like I have."

She turns to him and, grasping his shoulders, holds him in an odd arm's-length embrace. "You're a good-hearted boy," she tells him. "That's a great gift. We all appreciate your generosity. But Francisco is very proud. So is Rodolfo. If they can accept your generosity, then perhaps you can accept their pride."

Tiempo Loco

In the middle of the afternoon, an army of clouds masses on the western horizon, invades Santo Domingo, and unleashes an artillery barrage of hailstones. Rick and the Romeros retreat to the living room, huddle, and exchange worried glances. The *small* hailstones are the size of marbles and quickly rip off half the leaves of the *pirul* tree. The large ones look like icy golf balls and clatter when they strike the roofs and the courtyard. The noise, which started like a distant drum roll, quickly intensifies to a roar. It sounds as if a huge machine is grinding up the whole town.

Then, as suddenly as the storm started, it stops. Everyone waits, sure a second attack is pending.

Nothing happens.

Julio opens the door and goes outside. Rick, Francisco, and Emiliana soon follow, stepping out into bright sunshine.

Bewildered, Rick looks up. There's scarcely a cloud in the sky. Yet balls of sparkling ice clutter the patio and everything in it, and six pigeons lie dead on the ground.

"Que tiempo tan loco," says Julio wearily. What crazy weather. "How are we going to—" He cuts himself short and sets to work sweeping up the fallen leaves.

Time Is Running Out

"Let's get together and do something," Ellen says when Rick phones her early in the evening from the corner *bodega.*

"Great," he tells her. "I'd really like that." He pictures going to *el centro* with her, maybe finding a nice little restaurant and getting a bite to eat. Now that her dad has decided he's trustworthy . . .

"How about tonight? Can you come over? We could watch a movie—we've got a ton to choose from. I also have a new project I want to show you. It's a sculpture I'm making of found objects. Little pieces of wood. Broken pottery. Some souvenirs I've picked up in town." She laughs a little self-consciously. "I guess I took what you said to heart . . . you know, how being an artist means figuring things out? What to make and how to make it?"

"That sounds really cool. I'd love to see it."

"So can you come?"

Rick almost says yes, then holds back. "I'm really sorry, but I can't. We're working on the house tonight."

"You're working at night?"

"We're setting up the supports to pour a concrete roof. The hailstorm messed up our schedule, so we're working till nine or ten to catch up. We have to get organized before the storms get any worse."

"Oh," she says.

Rick can't tell if she's unconvinced by his explanation or merely disappointed. "I know it's not a great situation," he says.

"I guess not."

"Unfortunately, that's what we're stuck with."

"I guess so." After a pause, she says, "Well, maybe tomorrow."

"Maybe," Rick repeats hesitantly. "But I'm afraid I won't know our schedule till then."

"I see."

"We're racing the clock."

There's silence on the line.

"Ellen—you still there?"

"Yeah."

He can tell she's annoyed. "I really want to be with you—"

"You sure about that?"

"Of course! Come on, Ellen."

"You always seem so busy."

"Well, I *am* busy. I'm helping build a house—"

"Twenty-four hours a day?"

Now it's Rick who is annoyed. "Just about! That's how it is right now. We've got to get through these construction tasks, and the rains are coming, and time is running out."

"Okay, okay. I understand," she says in a flat tone.

"Thanks."

"I really do."

"I appreciate that."

"Call me when your schedule opens up."

"I will. I promise."

When they hang up, Rick stands in the phone booth a moment, listening to the radio blaring a Mexican love song and trying hard not to feel angry. But he *is* angry—at *la obra* for being so difficult, at the weather for delaying the construction schedule, at the Romeros for needing his help, at Ellen for not understanding what he's up against, and at life for being too damn complicated.

III

Bells Again

A single bell tolls, a mournful, somber sound. *What does it mean?* Rick wonders. *Has someone died? Or does it signal a Mass at just one church?* It's odd to hear such a solitary sound here; Santo Domingo is a town where noises usually arrive in overlapping waves.

Rick is stuffing little wads of newspaper between the squares of *cimbra,* sealing the cracks so that concrete won't ooze through during the *colado.* It's easy work that requires little concentration, and the bell he hears, its single note rolling over the town, leaves him hypnotized. Somehow it captures each moment, traps it, and preserves it like a bug in amber. Rick finds that he can't imagine doing anything but what he's doing now; he doesn't *want* to do anything else, and he can't believe he ever has. He has always sat up here, feeling the warm breeze on his neck, smelling the aroma of tortillas wafting up from Emiliana's kitchen, feeling the crinkle of the newsprint and the grain of the wood at his fingertips, hearing the endless toll of that lone, low, slow bell.

Flying Lessons

Rick sits on the patio steps with Hilaria. Her forehead is still bandaged, but the swelling has gone down, and she seems untroubled by her recent misadventure. Now she cheerfully demonstrates the proper technique for flying *mayates*. Three of the iridescent green beetles wait inside a glass jar resting on the step between them—along with a spool of Emiliana's thread.

"Aquí mero se le pone el hilo," Hilaria explains in her lilting voice. You put the thread on him right here. With her tiny fingers, she loops the thread around the bug's thorax.

Rick, gently holding the *mayate,* marvels at the girl's precise movements.

She sighs. "I don't know how to tie the knot. Remedios does that part for me."

"I'll do it," Rick assures her. Yet when he lets go, easing his grasp on the insect to pick up the thread, the *mayate* makes a sudden electrical noise—*bzzzzt!*—and flies away.

He expects Hilaria to be upset, but her reaction is altogether different: loud laughter. *"¡Tú no sabes cómo!"* she shouts. You don't know how!

Annoyed, Rick challenges her. "All right, so teach me."

"I'm trying."

"Try harder."

"Well, *you* try harder."

They set to work again. This time Hilaria holds the bug while Rick attempts to secure the tether. Fumbling with fingers that seem too big for the task, he finally succeeds, but the thread is so tight that the insect refuses to fly. In fact, his overzealous efforts may even have injured it.

"No sirve," Hilaria states gloomily. It's no good.

"Don't give up yet. We have one last chance."

Hilaria removes the third *mayate* from the jar and sets it on her knee. The bug rests there placidly, making no effort to escape, while she unwinds a length of thread and bites it free from the spool. This time, Rick ties the knot first, a tiny slipknot. Then Hilaria manages to ease the little noose under the wings and around the *mayate's* thorax without damaging any of the bug's delicate parts. She slides the knot into place. The *mayate* is now captive yet free to fly.

As if on cue, it takes off, buzzing dreamily, and hovers just a foot away from Hilaria, as docile as an old dog on a leash.

"Así se hace," she states. That's how it's done.

More Vocabulary

Rick isn't sure how to talk to the Romeros about Ellen. They now accept her presence in his life, but they don't really understand how much she matters to him. He's also had trouble explaining his relationship with them to her. Maybe if she comes for a visit, everything will stabilize. The Romeros will get to know her, she'll get to know them, and everyone will relax.

Rick riffles through his dictionary of standard Spanish and compiles a list of words and phrases to help him talk to the Romeros: *enamorarse de*—to fall in love with; *amante*—lover, beloved.

That's overstating the relationship, he decides, crossing out the words. He needs something more subtle. He checks his little dictionary of Mexican slang and adds to his list: *querida*—loved one; *novia*—girlfriend; *andar de volada*—to flirt.

He x's out this batch of words, too. Nothing seems to be serving his purposes. He keeps looking. *Enredarse con*—to get tangled up with, netted with; *amor brujo*—to be bewitched; *hacer el amor*—to make love.

Oh, perfect! Just what he needs.

Exasperated, Rick slaps the dictionaries shut and tosses his notebook to the floor. Maybe there's no good way to explain Ellen to the Romeros. He'll just have to take his chances and hope for the best.

Meeting the Family

"I'm not so sure about this," Ellen says as Rick leads her down the hill from her fancy *colonia* into the Romeros' neighborhood. She glances around in alarm, as if trying to spot a possible escape route.

Rick wonders if it's the messiness of the barrio that troubles her—the narrow *callejón,* the rocky dirt path, the crude houses, the trash littering the place. Or maybe it's the attention she has attracted. She's dressed in a curve-hugging pale blue T-shirt and white shorts, clothes that would go unnoticed back home but that, Rick knows, few teenage girls in small-town Mexico would ever wear. Some boys playing soccer stop kicking the ball and stare. Two teenage girls hanging out in a doorway lean close together and start whispering. Three men on a corner watch as Rick and Ellen walk by.

Rick greets everyone they encounter, and most people answer politely, but Ellen still looks nervous. "This place gives me the creeps," she says. "Isn't there a better way to get where we're going?"

"This *is* where we're going," he tells her.

"You're kidding."

A few minutes later they arrive at the Romeros' house and enter the patio. Now everything will settle down, he decides. They'll share the midday meal. The Romeros will charm Ellen. She will charm them. Everyone will get along.

But Ellen seems more uneasy, not less so, when she meets the Romeros. The introductions go badly. Rick has coached her to respond by saying, *"Mucho gusto"*—with great pleasure. But instead she says, *"Muchos gastos"*—many expenses. Rick also told her that most Mexicans shake hands gently, but Ellen automatically uses her powerful American-style grip, startling the Romeros. Everyone smiles and pretends there's no problem. Ellen's grin, however, looks tense and strained.

The only smooth interaction occurs between Ellen and Hilaria, who's present to help her aunt serve dinner. She stares with open fascination at *la gringa*. Is it Ellen's red-gold hair or lovely green eyes that draw her gaze? Or is it simply seeing this new American in the household so unexpectedly? Rick can't tell, but he's pleased to see the two of them smiling at each other.

"Hola," Ellen says.

"Hola," answers Hilaria, clearly delighted.

"*¿Quieren refrescos?*" asks Emiliana, motioning toward the kitchen.

"She's offering us something to drink," Rick tells Ellen. Then, noting her quick, longing glance up the hill toward *la colonia americana,* he decides that they might do better to stay outside for a while.

"*¿Qué piensas si le mostramos la obra?*" he asks the Romeros. What do you think about showing her the project?

"Good idea," says Julio. "She can see what keeps you so busy."

"What's going on?" Ellen asks anxiously.

"We're going to give you the grand tour."

Hilaria starts to lead the way, but Emiliana gently corrals her and takes her off to the kitchen. Francisco and Julio head up the ramp to the second floor. Rick gestures for Ellen to go ahead, then follows her. They gather inside the first of the two upper rooms, which now contain a small forest of vertical support beams. It's dark in there; the *vigas* and *cimbra* have capped the rooms with a tight lid.

"Wow, this place is built like a bunker!" she exclaims, running a hand along a wall.

"That's not accidental," Rick says. "Mexico is an earthquake zone, so houses have to be solid." He speaks in English but translates his comments into Spanish for Francisco and Julio.

"It's true," says Francisco. "A weak structure won't hold up."

Julio nods. "I've known people who have built skimpy houses, then regretted it when the ground started to shake."

Rick translates for Ellen, who nods in turn.

"What's all this?" She gestures at the beams.

"It's a platform to support the roof we'll be pouring," Rick explains. "This structure will hold the concrete in place while it dries."

"Clever."

"Once it's hard enough, we'll remove the beams and boards. Then we'll have a huge, solid roof."

Ellen spots a ladder propped up against the wall. "May I?"

Julio and Francisco glance with concern at one another.

"She'll be all right," Rick assures them. He knows how fit she is, and he doesn't want to disrupt her now that she's starting to relax. "Go ahead," he tells her.

She climbs the ladder without hesitation. Rick follows. Julio and Francisco climb up, too. Soon they're all standing on the upper surface of the squares of *cimbra*.

"Is it safe to walk on?" asks Ellen.

"If it can hold tons of concrete," says Rick, "I expect it'll support us."

Stepping carefully, making sure not to trip on the network of steel rebar, Ellen begins to cross the roof. "What are the metal rods for?" she asks.

Francisco grasps the question and answers without waiting for Rick's translation. "It's a grid of steel reinforcements to make the concrete stronger."

Rick passes on the explanation in English.

"Makes sense," says Ellen.

She leads the way across the *cimbra* to the outer room and gazes across the valley. Julio and Francisco say nothing. Perhaps they're giving Rick space to share the moment with her, or perhaps they're just feeling shy. But Rick is silent, too, mostly to see Ellen's response to the vista.

She stares for a long time, then says, "Wow."

Rick grins. "I've taken a lot of pictures from up here. Nice, isn't it?"

"This view is even better than ours."

Rick translates Ellen's last comment to Francisco and Julio, who nod in acknowledgment.

She gazes outward for a while before returning her attention to the Romeros' property. Rick can see her sizing up the place: the structure they're standing on, the patio below, the two rooms on the other side. "You guys built this whole thing?" Ellen asks, as if she's slightly in shock.

"Not bad, huh?" Rick says.

"Not bad at all!"

"*¿Qué le parece?*" Julio asks. What does she think?

"*Le gusta su casa,*" Rick replies. She likes your house.

"You're gossiping about me," says Ellen.

"Not really." First he thinks she's annoyed; then he sees the hint of a smile on her face.

"Tell them I think it's wonderful."

Soon it's time for dinner. Emiliana calls them from below in her high voice, and Francisco acknowledges with "*¡Ahorita!*" In a moment! Then the four of them work their way down from the roof.

By the time they arrive at the kitchen, Rick can see that Ellen is tensing up again. He can only hope that the Romeros' warmth, along with the pleasures of Emiliana's cooking, will soon put her at ease.

Emiliana has prepared a feast for the occasion. There's *sopa de lima,* "lime soup," which is really chicken stew with vegetables. Next a salad arrives, full of avocado slices and tiny tomatoes. Ellen eats contentedly but looks restless, no doubt because she doesn't understand the conversation. Then Emiliana and Hilaria serve the main course, *mole poblano de guajalote*—turkey in a rich, dark *mole* sauce that has been simmering since yesterday. Emiliana clearly has gone to enormous trouble—the equivalent of fixing a full Thanksgiving dinner for an honored guest. Along with the turkey there's rice, fried plantains, sautéed spinach, and fat little tortillas stuffed with squash. It's an amazing meal, and Rick is eager to dig in. Looking at Ellen, though, he realizes that she feels uncomfortable about the food arrayed before them. She told him once that she likes Mexican food, but some of these dishes are clearly unfamiliar to her.

"You okay?" he asks.

"Fine," she answers flatly.

"Don't feel you have to eat everything," he tells her. "Just try things."

"Right."

"Pues, ¡ándele!" Emiliana urges everyone. Well, go ahead!

Ellen cuts a small piece of turkey and tastes it warily.

Hilaria watches, rapt, as if a gringa eating dinner is the most remarkable sight on earth.

The Romeros start in eagerly. Julio is especially animated, eating fast and telling a story about one of his trips to Texas. "So remember how I found work on a chicken ranch? It's a big place, quite an operation, and the boss is kind to us. He's American, but he speaks excellent Spanish. 'Make yourselves comfortable, fellows. Work hard, and I'll do good things for you,' he says. 'And if you're hungry, grab a chicken, kill it, and roast it yourselves.' Just like that—'Roast it yourselves!'"

Rick is watching Ellen. She looks uneasy, but he's not sure if it's the rich *mole* sauce or something else that's causing her discomfort.

"Well, believe me," says Julio, "we ate chicken every day. We ate chicken every *meal*. In a few weeks, we all sprouted feathers!"

Everyone laughs—Francisco, Emiliana, Hilaria, Rick, even Julio himself. As it happens, the whole group is looking toward Ellen at that moment. Rick knows this is just a coincidence, but the timing is unfortunate.

Ellen turns to him and says, "I have to go."

"What's wrong?"

"I have to go *now*." She pushes back her chair without meeting his gaze.

"Is anything the matter?" asks Emiliana.

Excusing the two of them, Rick follows Ellen out of the kitchen and into the alley. "They weren't laughing at you," he tells her.

"They were *too* laughing!"

"But not at *you!* Julio was telling a funny story about working on a chicken ranch."

"I want to go home."

"Ellen, please don't go."

She gazes at him silently.

He keeps thinking she'll head up the hill and leave, but she doesn't. Maybe he can persuade her to stay ... "Please don't misinterpret what happened. They *like* you," he tells her. "And I promise that from now on, I'll translate everything they say."

Only with great reluctance does she agree to rejoin the dinner table.

Leave Your Name and Number

Later, once Rick has returned Ellen to the Bradshaws' house and he's back at work, he ponders why the visit went so badly. Ellen felt embarrassed because she acted like a jerk, as she put it; the Romeros were ashamed because they felt they weren't sufficiently hospitable. Now Rick finds himself caught in the middle. Trying to make things better, he has only made them worse.

He's tempted to call Ellen but holds off. She's feeling pressured. She needs time to calm down. Then, deciding that silence is a mistake, he phones her that evening.

The answering machine picks up. "You have reached the offices of Cybernexus," states Mr. Bradshaw's recorded voice. "We can't speak with you just now, but we'll return your call if you'll leave your name and number."

"Ellen, this is Rick," he says, trying to keep his voice steady. "Can you pick up?"

There's no response.

He falters, then says, "Everything's fine. The Romeros really like you. *I really like you.*" After a moment's hesitation he adds, "Let's get together, okay?"

It's no wonder she got spooked, Rick thinks as he hangs up the phone. *I should have prepared her better. I should have told her what to expect.* He recalls his early days with the Romeros—how new and strange and confusing everything was then. And he'd had the advantage of speaking *some* Spanish at least.

Standing there in the *bodega,* he's struck by how long ago it seems that he arrived in Santo Domingo.

Disaster

The next day, while walking down the ramp that extends from the second floor to the patio, Julio loses his footing. He falls, striking his left side against the ramp, and drops eight feet to the kitchen stoop. Rick is in the patio and witnesses the accident. One second Julio is up on the ramp; the next he's on the ground.

"Oh, my god!" Rick yells, racing over. "Emiliana! Francisco!"

Emiliana rushes out to the kitchen. Francisco appears a second later. They're screaming and jolting into each other as they reach Julio's side.

"*¡Ay, Dios mío, Dios mío!*"

"*¡Papi, Papi—háblame!*"

"Julio!"

Julio lies flat on his back, staring straight up. His eyes have bugged out, and his mouth seems frozen in a scream that somehow can't escape from his throat. He doesn't move. He doesn't even breathe.

Please, please, Rick begs. *Don't let him be dead!*

Emiliana rests her forehead on her husband's chest. *"No me dejes, no me dejes,"* she wails. Don't leave me, don't leave me.

Francisco alternately strokes his dad's head and slaps him gently on the cheek.

Then Julio utters a bizarre sound—a long, gravelly *ahhh . . .* He suddenly curls up, rolling onto his left side, then starts gasping for breath.

"Is there an ambulance in Santo Domingo?" Rick asks. "We have to get him to the clinic."

"Yes, I'll go call," Francisco yells, and races off toward the *bodega.*

The ambulance arrives in ten or twelve minutes, though it seems like hours, and parks at the end of Callejón Hidalgo. Then the EMTs bring a stretcher to the house and carry Julio down the alley. Emiliana climbs into the back of the ambulance with Julio, and it heads off to the clinic. Francisco and Rick hurry down on foot. By the time the two of them reach their destination, Julio is in the emergency room. They join Emiliana in the hallway outside.

"The doctor and the nurses are with him," she tells them, then she falls silent. Sitting bolt upright in the only chair, she stares with tear-rimmed eyes at the opposite wall. Rick and Francisco stand on either side of her but don't speak. The closed door muffles the voices, so Rick can't understand what's being said. Now and then he hears a deep, guttural moan that makes his back and neck tingle in sympathy.

A long time passes—forty minutes . . . an hour . . . maybe more. Rick loses track. *What will happen if Julio is severely injured . . . if he dies? How will the Romero family survive?* He shakes his head, trying to dispel the thoughts.

Suddenly the door opens. A young woman in a flowered dress and white lab coat steps into the hallway.

Emiliana stands at once. *"¿Doctora?"*

The doctor smiles at her. "Your husband is out of danger, señora Romero."

"Gracias a Dios," Emiliana says, and she starts to cry.

While Francisco comforts his mother, Dr. Jiménez explains the situation. Julio appears to have no organ damage, but x-rays show that he has broken several ribs. She has taped his rib cage, to stabilize the fractures. There's not much else that she can do for him. "I'll prescribe some painkillers," she tells Emiliana, "but I'm afraid your husband will be in discomfort for many weeks."

"He'll be okay?"

"He has avoided severe injury, but he's going to feel awful."

Making the sign of the cross, Emiliana thanks God and the doctor. "May I see him?" she asks.

"Please come in."

Emiliana and Francisco follow Dr. Jiménez into the room. Rick stays outside to give the family some privacy, but they leave the door open, and he can see and overhear what follows. To his surprise, Emiliana doesn't break down again; she simply stands beside her husband and gently takes his right hand.

Julio touches the swath of tape on his left side and gazes up miserably at his wife. Then, flinching with every word, he asks the doctor, "Can I work?"

"What's your profession, señor Romero?"

"I'm a bricklayer."

"Oh, my lord—I'm afraid not."

"I need to work."

"It's out of the question," she states firmly.

"We have a big *colado* we're trying to finish before the rainy season."

Dr. Jiménez gestures in exasperation. "Señor Romero, you nearly broke your back today. It's going to take months for your ribs to heal. Please don't push your luck."

Rick pays the bill without even asking if this is okay. Then a taxi takes everyone back to the barrio. Julio tries to act upbeat about his brush with disaster. *"No es gran cosa."* It's no big deal. But Rick can tell he's in great pain. Every time the taxi hits a bump, he hears Julio gasp. Then, once they reach the corner of Hidalgo and Aparicio, the really difficult part of the trip begins. It takes Rick and Francisco, supporting Julio on either side, almost fifteen minutes to walk the one block to the Romeros' house.

As they descend the stairs into the patio, Julio glances at all the materials and equipment piled there and groans. *"Pues, ¿cómo acabamos?"* he says. So, how are we going to finish?

Exactly, Rick thinks.

Out of Control

"Thank God Julio is okay," Rick's father says after Rick has explained the situation by phone that evening. "But what a disaster. It seems this project has been one problem after another."

Rick is frustrated by his dad's reaction, and by his mom's, too, since she has fallen completely silent. "Gee, thanks for the support," he mutters.

"I'm not criticizing," Dad says. "I'm just concerned."

"Well, I'm concerned, too."

"You're dealing with all sorts of issues. Misunderstandings. Money troubles. And now this accident—"

"I'm doing the best I can!" Rick blurts.

"Of course you are," Mom says. "We know you've tried hard."

"But sometimes plans simply don't work out," Dad adds.

"Give me a break, will you?" Rick demands. "I just need some time to figure things out." He and the Romeros have worked so hard for so long, and they've come so far. He can't accept the fact that the whole project might just grind to a halt, and somehow his parents haven't grasped this or understood how upset it makes him.

"Is it really wise to keep pushing?" Dad says. "Because it seems to me—"

Suddenly Mom interrupts. "Sweetie, I think you should come home."

"What?" Rick can't believe what he's heard.

"There's nothing wrong with cutting your stay a little short," Dad says. "You've given it your best. Let's admit we all miscalculated. The project has gotten out of control."

"It *hasn't!*" Rick shouts, startling the people waiting outside his booth at Teléfonos de México. "It's *not* out of control! We *didn't* miscalculate!"

His parents must be upset or shocked or both by his reaction. Whatever they're feeling, they are silent. There's a sequence of tiny digital bleeps on the line, followed by a faint hiss. That's when he realizes that no matter what they say, he's made up his mind. He won't give up. He's not going to let Julio's accident doom the project.

"Hello?" he says, his voice calmer now.

"We're here," Mom says.

"Sorry. I didn't mean to yell."

"It's okay."

"I just want you to know—we're going to do this," he tells his parents. "We're going to finish the house. I don't care what else happens, we're going to finish."

Pleading the Case

All the next morning, people come and go from the Romeros' house—Emiliana's sister Carmen; Julio's brother Aniseto; Antonia,

Rodolfo, and the two little ones; neighbors—all concerned about how Julio is doing. He seems to enjoy the attention, but Rick can see it's difficult for him to sit for so long. At last Emiliana shoos everyone off, and Julio goes to lie down. Then she and Hilaria start in on a cleaning project, and Francisco heads out to try to find workers for the *colado*.

Rick decides to visit Ellen. He can't do any construction work alone. Besides, there's something on his mind, something he wants to discuss with her. He calls from the *bodega,* finds her home, and tells her about the accident. She's concerned and attentive—and happy to have him come for a visit.

"I'm not sure what we'll do, now that Julio is out of commission," Rick tells Ellen as they sit beside the pool after a long swim. "If we can't lay down the concrete roof soon, the whole project might be wrecked."

"Can't it wait till he's better?"

"No, not with the rains already starting." Rick watches sunlight twist and contort on the water's surface. It's hard to imagine anything as disruptive as a rainy season in this calm, beautiful place.

"Well, maybe they can wait till the rainy season is over, then pick up where they left off."

"They need to do it now," Rick tells her. "Once the rains finish, it'll be too late. I'll be gone. Francisco may be in school. They won't have enough people."

"I'm sorry about all that," she says. "I like your friends, and I think what they're doing is cool. I hope things work out for them."

Rick turns and smiles at her. "Maybe you could do more than hope."

She looks puzzled. "What do you mean?"

"I'd really like your help."

"On the *project*?" she asks, clearly startled.

"Yes," he says simply.

She doesn't respond, but he decides not to give up. "Look. You say you're bored. You say you want to make stuff. Well, here's your chance. Think of the house as a giant sculpture."

"I've never done construction work."

"Neither had I until the Romeros showed me how. You'd learn quickly."

"I don't know about that . . ." Ellen shakes her head. She looks uncomfortable.

"Just give it a try," he says. "Come and see what you think. If you decide not to take part, no big deal. Everyone will understand."

She's silent for a long time. Then she says, "How much concrete?"

"You don't want to know. Tons and tons."

"How does a cement truck get up that skinny little street?"

"It doesn't. We mix the concrete ourselves—by hand."

"By hand?"

"In batches."

"Jeez—I'm not sure I'm really up for that."

"You'll love it, I promise! It's even messier than throwing pots, and the results are a whole lot bigger."

"This is so crazy."

"Ellen . . ."

She shakes her head. "Look, I'm sure the Romeros are wonderful, but I hardly know them."

"Don't do it for them. Do it for me."

"I'm sorry," she says. "I'd like to, but I can't. It's something . . . I just can't."

Storms

Clouds mass to the west, overwhelming the town within minutes. Rain falls, then hail, then still more rain. During the hailstorm, marble-sized chunks of ice hammer at the second floor's wooden platform of *vigas* and *cimbra,* creating a noise like a jet preparing for takeoff.

The Romeros and Rick huddle in the new downstairs room. Francisco has stuck some boards in the empty window, so nothing enters the room but a small amount of seepage under the door. Still, everyone seems demoralized. No one speaks. They drink coffee and listen to the blast of water and ice striking wood, brick, and concrete overhead.

Having grown up near the Rocky Mountains, Rick is familiar with rough weather. This storm doesn't come close to the most violent ones he's witnessed. Yet it seems more dangerous because there's less protection here. Back home, he'd be listening to the wind and rain in a modern house with central heating and double-paned windows. Here there's no furnace, no weather-sealed door, not even glass in the window frames. It's easy to feel vulnerable.

"What's today?" asks Julio.

Francisco checks the calendar. "August twentieth," he answers.

"When is your plane flight home?" Emiliana asks Rick. "The thirtieth?"

"The twenty-ninth," he answers.

"*Ay,*" is her only answer.

It Wasn't Worth the Trouble

Late the next morning, Rick is standing at the courtyard water faucet, washing his face, when the doorbell clanks twice. Julio, who sits nearby, starts to get up, but Hilaria scampers to answer it, then cries out in surprise. Two people enter the Romeros' house, with Hilaria practically dancing around them.

"*¿Qué tal, Tío?*" one of them calls out. How's it going, Uncle?

It's Alfonso and Lucho. Both are sunburned—especially Lucho, whose mottled skin is raw pink on the pale patches—but both seem cheerful and energetic.

Julio gives them a big smile. "*Pues, ¿qué pasó, chavos?*" Well, what happened, guys?

"*Nada,*" says Alfonso. Nothing.

"*Nadita,*" says Lucho. Absolutely nothing.

"You're back so soon!" Francisco exclaims, joining the group. At once he starts teasing. "Did you miss the bus? Did you forget to board when they announced the departure?"

"*¿Qué sabes tú de autobuses, Primo?*" Lucho shoots back. What do you know about buses, Cousin?

"You've never even traveled across town," Alfonso adds.

The boys reach out and hug Francisco. They hug Julio as well, though carefully, patting him on his right shoulder. They don't mention his injury, but part of the bandage is visible, so they're clearly aware of it.

Emiliana emerges from the kitchen. She's smiling, but Rick can see tears on her cheeks. *"Muchachos . . . muchachos . . . ,"* she says, unable to say more.

After hugging their aunt, Alfonso and Lucho nod politely in Rick's direction, then study the changes in the courtyard.

"Se ve bien la obra," says Lucho. The project looks good.

"Ya merito acabamos," Julio replies. Pretty soon we'll finish.

Rick expects Julio to say more, to ask the guys to help with the *colado,* but he doesn't go on.

"You'll have dinner with us," Emiliana says—stating a fact, not asking a question.

What happened, the boys explain, was that their trip *al norte* ended almost as soon as it began. Alfonso, Lucho, and Juan reached the border as planned, and they fell in with a large group of other *mojados.* They waited till dark, swarmed over a chainlink fence, scrambled down to the river, and waded across. The U.S. immigration police were right on the other side and caught most members of the group. Lucho and Alfonso got separated from Juan and spent the night in a detention center before getting bused back across the border. They made a second attempt two days later but got lost in the desert for almost forty-eight hours. Then they were caught again. At this point they simply gave up.

"No valió la pena," says Lucho. It wasn't worth the trouble.

"Y aquí estamos," adds Alfonso. And here we are.

"Well, I'm glad," Julio tells them.

Everyone sitting at the table looks pleased—most of all Hilaria, who stares at her brothers with an expression of hungry delight.

"And you, Uncle," says Lucho. "What's all this?" He gestures at the expanse of tape visible on the crest of Julio's shoulder.

Julio looks puzzled. "This? Nothing."

"Did you criticize Auntie's cooking?"

"No way—I just had a little slip."

"He had a little slip," says Emiliana, "and *I* had a little heart attack."

"I'll be fine," says Julio, brushing off his near-catastrophe with a laugh.

Emiliana shoots him an irritable glance. "Not if you keep pushing your luck."

"So, how's the project?" asks Alfonso.

"Fine."

"No problems?" asks Lucho. He nods toward *la obra.* "Still on schedule?"

"More or less."

"Everything's going well?"

"Just great."

Rick isn't sure what's going on. He knows that the Romeros were sad when the guys left, and they're visibly relieved to have them back. Surely they're also pleased that Alfonso and Lucho can now help with the *colado.* So why isn't Julio *saying* something about it? *"Ask* them!" he wants to shout.

Emiliana apparently feels the same way. "What don Julio is telling you," she says, speaking to Alfonso and Lucho but staring in annoyance at her husband, "is that we're desperate for your assistance. Can you help us?"

Alfonso and Lucho glance at each other, then simultaneously guffaw.

"*Pues, claro,*" says Alfonso. Well, of course.

El Gran Colado

Francisco didn't succeed in recruiting other workers, so they're still short two men. Six would make for a long day of hard work. Five might let them squeak through and complete the job. Four simply isn't enough. This should rule out proceeding, but Julio decides to gamble and go ahead. The weather is deteriorating. Rick will be gone in seven days. Francisco may be starting his studies at the teachers' college. And who knows? Maybe Alfonso and Lucho will head off to Texas again. It seems better to attempt *el gran colado* under less than promising conditions than to lose the chance altogether.

Rick and the Romeros wake up well before sunrise on the twenty-second and eat a quick breakfast. Alfonso and Lucho show up a few minutes later, shivering in the predawn chill. Julio maps out the strategy.

"Here's what we'll do," he says. "Ordinarily we'd have two guys mixing, two carrying, and two laying concrete. I'm out of the picture, though, so we'll do things differently. You're going to take turns doing each job. That way, none of you will get tired doing any one thing. All the tasks are difficult, but they're difficult in different ways."

Rick and the other guys nod in assent. No one interrupts or asks questions, as if conserving energy for the ordeal ahead.

"You'll make the first batch of concrete together. For two hours, Lucho and Ricardo will carry it up in *botes* while Alfonso and Francisco settle it into place. Then you'll switch for two hours. Then you'll switch again, back and forth, over and over. Got it?"

"Yes, Uncle."

"Right, Papi."

"Got it, Julio."

Emiliana speaks up. "If you need something to drink, just yell. The same if you need food. The same if you need me to pound on your back to get the kinks out."

"Even if we're lucky," says Julio, "we'll be working all day and half the night."

Rick takes a deep breath. He can't imagine how they'll pull this off. But if they fail, it won't be for lack of trying. He's determined to give it every ounce of his strength.

"*¿Listos?*"

Everyone nods.

"*Vámonos.*"

The first batch goes well, since all four guys collaborate in mixing it. Rick is stiff at first—he hasn't done such hard work in over a week—but he quickly limbers up, and exerting himself allows him to shake off the morning chill. He's pleased by how strong he feels and by how easily the concrete surrenders to his shovel. Maybe this *colado* won't be so bad after all. They'll throw the roof together! They'll be done in no time! As the shovels clank and the concrete sputters and slurps, he starts to feel more confident about what they're doing.

But hauling the stuff forces him to realize how difficult the job will be. First he shovels enough concrete to fill a *bote*. Then, hoisting it onto his right shoulder, he climbs the patio stairs to the ramp. From there it's a short walk up the ramp to the second-floor landing. Then he ties the handle of the *bote* to a rope, which either Alfonso or Francisco hauls up to the second-floor roof. He performs this sequence many times. Three dozen? Four dozen? It's hard to keep track, and doing so would be pointless, anyway, making the work seem harder than it already is.

"*¿Qué tal?*" he calls up to Francisco at one point.

"*Bien. Poco a poco,*" Francisco tells him. Fine. Little by little.

They use up the first batch of concrete. While mixing the second, Rick glances at his watch. It's only seven—earlier than he ordinarily wakes up. He thought it was midmorning, at least. But what does it matter? All he can do is keep going, churning cement, sand, gravel, and water into concrete, then hauling it up to the roof.

Soon it's time for Rick and Lucho to switch places with Alfonso and Francisco. They climb the ladder to the roof, and Rick almost shouts in dismay. So little of the expanse has received its share of the cement; in fact, just the far corner.

Before Rick can say anything, however, Francisco starts explaining what he and Lucho are supposed to do. "Here's how it works. Lucho, let's say you bring over a *bote* full of concrete. You dump it there"—Francisco points to the ragged edge of the *colado*—"then, Ricardo, you take your trowel and settle it in. Make sure it spreads and gets under the rebar. Stab it to pop any air pockets. Then, once there's enough concrete to cover the rebar, smooth out the surface."

Within a few minutes of hearing this explanation, everyone is back at work. Rick and Lucho take turns with the rope and the trowel. This allows them to alternate the effort of hauling up the buckets with the discomfort of squatting on the rebar and *cimbra*. Neither job is much easier than what Rick had been doing earlier. In fact, in some ways, they're harder, because they exert more strain on the back, knees, and arms. Working up on the roof also shows Rick how little progress they're making—and that's hard, too.

They've just switched jobs again when Rodolfo shows up. He's dressed like his brothers, in jeans and T-shirt, but he sports a cowboy hat and carries his guitar.

"*¡Quiúbole, chavos!*" he says. What's up, guys!

"*¡Supersobrino al rescate!*" Julio shouts amiably. Super Nephew to the rescue!

"I'm going to help out," Rodolfo announces.

"*Sure* you are," Francisco calls down from the roof.

Rodolfo seats himself carefully on the steps that descend from the kitchen to the patio. He strums a few chords. "Any requests?"

"Yeah," says Francisco. "Pull the door shut as you leave."

"Now, now. A *colado* needs a little background music."

He starts playing, but Rick and the others ignore him. No one has the time or energy to deal with Rodolfo.

Emiliana appears in the kitchen doorway. "How's your mother?" she asks.

"Not feeling well."

"Any news from your dad?"

"No." Rodolfo smiles sweetly at his aunt. "How about fixing me some breakfast?"

"How about doing a little work?"

"No, thanks," he says. "I'm not *that* hungry."

On and on, the work goes. On and on. Around ten, Hilaria arrives to help Emiliana prepare and serve a snack: lemonade and fried-egg sandwiches. Everyone takes a break. Rick guzzles the lemonade and devours his sandwich. The food helps, though he notices that his hands have started to tremble from muscle strain.

"¿Estás bien, gringuito?" asks Hilaria. Are you okay, little gringo?

"Estoy bien," he tells her. I'm fine.

"Are you sure?" asks Julio, looking concerned.

"I'm fine. I just needed a breather."

"Take longer, if you like."

Emiliana intervenes. "We'd like you to rest."

Rick sees that the others have already started piling sand, cement, and gravel in the patio to make the next batch of concrete. He isn't going to humiliate himself by slacking off. "No—I'm ready," he insists, and he heads back to work.

"I'm not sure how we'll manage to pull this off," Julio says just before noon. "You guys are doing a great job, but we're only one-fourth finished, and—understandably—you're starting to lose energy and slow down."

"Sorry, Uncle," says Lucho.

Julio shoves him gently. "It's not *your* fault, it's *mine*. What an idiot I was to slip and fall."

"Don't blame yourself, Papi," Francisco says. "Let's just do what we can."

Emiliana asks, "You boys need some food?"

"Just something to drink, Auntie," Alfonso tells her.

While Hilaria fetches cups, everyone else simply stands around. No one speaks. Everyone looks discouraged, as if their efforts have already failed.

They fill the cups from the courtyard water faucet and drink deeply, then prepare to resume work. Trying to stretch his weary muscles, Rick wanders around the patio.

A voice catches his attention—someone speaking from beyond the wall, standing in Callejón Hidalgo.

"—looking for the Romeros."

It's a feminine voice, a voice he recognizes.

"*Aquí mero*," says a second voice. Right here.

Rick bounds up the patio steps and pulls open the front door just as the bell rings.

On the other side, looking surprised, is Ellen. She's wearing sneakers, jeans, and a yellow T-shirt with *Cybernexus—Your Connection to Tomorrow* printed on the front.

"Oh," she says.

"You're here?" he asks, startled.

"Well—yeah."

Rick's head is swimming. "Hey, it's great to see you, and I'd love to visit," he says, "but we're in the middle of the *colado*."

She dangles a pair of work gloves before him and smiles.

"For me?" Rick asks.

"No, goofball." She steps past him. "For *me*."

Ellen creates quite a stir—all the more so when Rick explains why she's there. "It's too dangerous," insists Emiliana. "It's too difficult," says Julio. Alfonso and Lucho seem baffled. Why would anyone, most of all a gringa, want to break her back on a *colado*? Rodolfo responds only by serenading Ellen. *"Déjame contarte cómo te adoro . . ."* Let me tell you how much I adore you . . .

Everyone stands around discussing the situation while Ellen waits. Only Hilaria makes her feelings evident. She's clearly excited that Ellen has arrived.

"What's the problem?" Ellen asks Rick.

"They're not sure if this is a good idea—you helping out, I mean."

"What? First you say they'll never make it without me! Now you say they don't think I should help?" She sounds more amazed than offended. Then, abruptly, she walks to the middle of the patio, grabs a shovel, and starts slopping concrete into a *bote*. She lifts it, clutches it to her chest, marches up the stairs and up the ramp, and waits near the ladder. "Well?" she says. "Where do I put this stuff?"

A Work of Art

Somehow the day's work is transformed. At first Rick isn't sure why. The team was formerly four workers; now it's five. Ellen is strong, steady, and cheerful, but her individual contribution in batches mixed, *botes* hauled, and concrete spread is no greater than anyone else's. So what makes the difference? Maybe it's the freedom granted by having an extra worker—the freedom for the crew to mix and haul concrete simultaneously. Or maybe it's something more intangible. Ellen's arrival has drawn new energy from each of them. Are the boys showing off for this pretty girl? Of course! No one wants to look weak in her eyes. Rick *knows* that's true for him. It even appears to be true for Rodolfo. He sets down his guitar, fills a *bote,* and takes the first of what becomes a long series of trips up the ramp.

Ellen also affects people other than the Romeros and their helpers. It seems that word of her presence has gotten around, because neighbors soon begin to stop by. Some are simply local kids who boost themselves up to peer over the wall bordering the *callejón.* Some are men who live nearby and show up out of curiosity, then actually pitch in for a while. Carmen brings a plate of chicken tacos and helps Emiliana in the kitchen. Hilaria fetches cups of water whenever the workers call out for a drink. At times, the whole place is full of people—the Mexican equivalent of a barn raising. At other times, the crowd thins, and Julio and his crew are alone again.

Rick isn't sure what accounts for the fluctuations or the big turnout. Are these residents of the barrio just curious about what two gringos are doing here? Or would any *colado* prompt as much interest? On some level, he doesn't care. He's just glad that some of them are sufficiently interested to help out.

Most of all, he's happy to have Ellen there with him—to have her fully involved in *la obra,* to work right beside her, to see her strength and confidence, to watch how her smiles and laughter lift everyone's spirits.

"So—what do you think?" he asks her at one point.

"Amazing," she says. "Just amazing."

The day grows warm, then hot, then cooler as the sun passes overhead. Refusing to take time off for a big meal, the Romeros and their assistants take only brief breaks for drinks and snacks. They mix, haul, and lay the concrete. The *colado* spreads like a dark shadow from west to east. The pace slows, falters, picks up again, falters once more. Each person takes turns doing all the tasks, though Ellen, by her own choice and by the others' request, spends most of her time stabbing the concrete into place, shaping it, smoothing its surface.

"She's good," Julio tells Rick at one point. "She's *really* good."

"Did you know she's an artist?" Rick asks. "She's a sculptor and potter."

"No kidding!"

"It's true."

"Well, that explains it," Julio says with pride. "Now this house is a work of art."

It's almost ten when they're finally done. Working in the dark, with only flashlights guiding them, they complete the roof—a huge, mud-scented expanse of concrete. Francisco and Ellen are stuck briefly on the nearest corner until Rick and Alfonso move the ladder a few feet, making it possible for them to descend. Then everyone stands around in the courtyard for a while, almost stunned by what they have accomplished.

"*Qué gran cosa han hecho,*" Julio tells them. What a great thing you've done. "I am so happy! So proud of all of you."

They take turns rinsing their hands with the garden hose. Everyone's clothes are crusted with concrete.

"Be sure to bathe, or you'll wake up solid as a rock," Emiliana tells Ellen. "Rinse out your jeans and T-shirt, too."

Rick translates.

Ellen smiles but seems too tired to speak. She reaches out to Emiliana and gives her a hug.

"*Gracias, jovencita,*" Emiliana tells her. Thank you, young woman.

The men shake hands with her shyly.

Rick and Ellen walk to the *bodega,* and he calls a cab to take her home. It's only a few minutes before it trundles up Calle Aparicio from *el centro.*

"Thanks," she tells him as she slides into the back seat. "This was really great."

"*You* were really great," he says, closing the door and leaning against the cab. "You saved the day. How can I ever thank you? What can I say?"

"Don't," she tells him. "Don't say anything at all." She leans through the open window and kisses him good night. "This was either the weirdest date I've ever had, or one of the best things I've ever done. Maybe both."

The cab pulls away.

Dizzy with fatigue and delight, Rick watches till it's out of sight. Then he jumps into the air, pumping his fist and shouting, "Yes!" so loudly that he startles the few people still out at such a late hour. He returns to Hidalgo, leaping and bounding all the way, then heads up the *callejón.* In the moonlight, the muddy cobbled lane looks more splendid and perfect than if it were paved with gold.

We Did It!

The next morning, Rick wakes up on the sofa in exactly the same position as when he collapsed there the night before. He can barely move. His shoulders, back, arms, and legs are as stiff as concrete. His hands and knees throb. Only with great effort does he manage to get up.

Despite his aches and pains, he's exhilarated. They pulled it off! They completed *el colado*! Tiptoeing past Francisco, who's still asleep on his mattress, Rick opens the door, to a sunny day outside—not a cloud in the sky, much less an impending storm that could damage the previous day's work.

He finds Julio and Emiliana, eating breakfast in the kitchen. *"Lo hicimos,"* he says proudly. We did it.

"Ustedes mismos lo hicieron. Yo no hice nada," Julio corrects him. You yourselves did it. I did nothing.

Rick says, *"No—nosotros juntos."* No—all of us together.

They argue amiably for a while, each trying to force the other to take credit. Then Emiliana says, *"Ricardo, nada más quiero agradecerte. Y dile gracias a la guapa también."* All I want to say is thank you. And tell the pretty girl thank you as well.

Later that morning, Rick tries phoning Ellen from the *bodega*. He gets a pickup, but it's only the Bradshaws' answering machine. *Ellen must still be sleeping,* he thinks. *She probably switched on the machine so she wouldn't be disturbed.*

When he returns to the house, he gets out his camera and takes pictures of *la obra* from all angles. Then he and Francisco scramble up the *pirul* tree and survey their handiwork. By daylight, it's even more impressive than it was the night before. The *colado* is enormous. The slate-gray, still-damp surface seems to extend for a dozen yards in one direction, two dozen yards in the other. Rick can't believe that they tackled such a huge job . . . tackled, accomplished, and completed.

"*¿Cómo se ve?*" Julio calls from below. How does it look?

"*¡A todo dar!*" Francisco calls down. Just great!

As Rick clambers down the slanted tree trunk, he notes with satisfaction that the pigeons have not made their mark on the *colado*. It's still as smooth and dark as the surface of a pond.

The News

The next day, Rick tries to reach Ellen again, without success. By now he's concerned. Is she all right? Did the work wear her out so much that she got sick? Is she upset about something?

He thinks about visiting her, but he's still tired enough that he doesn't relish the idea of walking up to *la colonia americana* and not finding her home. So he waits awhile and then calls again. To his delight, she picks up right away.

"How are you doing? I'm so glad to reach you," he says. "Come and see how the work turned out. It looks absolutely great!"

"I can't," she states in a flat tone of voice.

"Maybe tomorrow, then."

"No—I mean ever."

Rick falters. The *bodega* is a noisy place, with people chatting and a radio playing, so perhaps he hasn't understood her right. "What did you say?"

"I can't visit you there. Or anywhere."

"Are you joking?"

"Dad grounded me for the rest of my stay."

"What!"

"I can't see you again."

Rick feels as if he's been punched in the gut. "Can't see me? *Why?*"

"Because of what we did. The work. The *colado.*"

"Your dad is ticked off because we did some construction work?"

"He says you exploited me and put me in a bad situation."

Rick is speechless. He's so surprised, he can't think clearly. He knows that Mr. Bradshaw is overprotective, but it doesn't seem possible that he'd so totally misinterpret what happened.

There's an interruption—a male voice speaking to Ellen. Rick can't hear the words clearly. Something muffles the conversation, probably Ellen's hand cupped over the receiver. But he can tell that the speaker is Mr. Bradshaw.

"Ellen?"

"I've gotta go," she states blankly.

"Ellen—"

"I can't talk with you."

"Wait a sec."

"Rick, I'm sorry."

The line goes dead.

He stands there for a long time, listening to the phone hum in his ear, as if by not hanging up he can somehow bring Ellen's voice back on the line.

Cleanup

There's still a lot of work to be done. Although the *colado* has set and appears to be drying well, Francisco and Rick spend some time spraying it down with the garden hose. Julio has explained that rewetting the concrete makes it dry more slowly, which creates a harder surface in the long run. Rick goes first; this is the easiest work he's done in ages. Then, while Francisco takes a turn, he stands and gazes at the view from the rooftop.

Francisco says little while he works. He's not talkative by nature, but today he seems unusually quiet.

"So, are you . . . pleased?" Rick asks him.

"With the *colado*?"

Rick hesitates. That's what he asked about, but perhaps the roof isn't the whole subject. He wonders, *If Francisco assumes we're talking about something else, what would that be?* But he knows he'll get no answer if he asks.

"Right," he says. "The *colado*."

"*Completamente.*"

"*¿Y la casa?*"

"Claro." Of course. The word carries more than a touch of irritation.

Rick can scarcely restrain himself. *What are you annoyed about?* he wants to ask. *Why are you angry with me?* But he doesn't. He simply watches Francisco checking the *colado* for cracks and spraying a wide fan of water onto the concrete surface.

Wonderful, Wonderful, Wonderful

"We did it!" Rick tells his parents the next time he calls home.

"You're finished?" his mom asks, amazed. "With the whole house?"

"With the roof—the really hard part," he replies. "There's still a lot to do, but it's nothing major."

"That's wonderful!" Mom says.

"Wonderful," Dad echoes. "Congratulations!"

Rick is pleased by their reaction, but his mind is buzzing with other emotions, too. He wants to tell them about the hassles with Ellen's dad. He wants to describe the tension between him and Francisco. He wants to explain all kinds of other things. But he doesn't know where to begin.

"How's Julio?" Mom asks.

"Better. Clearly on the mend."

"He didn't work on this last phase, did he?" Dad asks.

"He didn't do any physical labor, but he definitely directed traffic."

"So all the problems got resolved," Dad says.

Well, not quite all *the problems,* thinks Rick. But he can't go into the complexities now. He'll explain everything later, when he's back home again . . . when he's had enough time to make sense of what's happened.

"Yeah," he says, "everything is wonderful."

A Heart-to-Heart

"This is strictly between me and my daughter," Ellen's father states over the intercom while Rick stands at the gated entrance to the Bradshaws' house. "As far as I'm concerned, you're irrelevant."

"May I just explain what happened?" Rick asks. He feels a wild mixture of emotions swirling through his body—anger, disgust, sorrow, and confusion. It's humiliating to plead his case to a black box mounted on a wall, but in his heart he knows he'll never have another chance.

"I have nothing more to say," says Mr. Bradshaw.

"Maybe *I* do."

"Oh? Well, that's of no concern to me."

"Mr. Bradshaw, this was all my fault. Not Ellen's. Mine."

The intercom is silent. Gazing through the wrought-iron gate, Rick can see every detail of the Bradshaws' house—massive and perfect in the intense sunlight—but he can't see any people. Are they watching him through the tinted windows? Is Ellen gazing at him while her dad makes sure he doesn't try sneaking in?

"I'd like to explain," Rick adds. "Please, Mr. Bradshaw."

More silence.

He's starting to feel ridiculous standing there. How long should he wait for a response? He doesn't want to miss this opportunity to set things right. But he also doesn't want to make Ellen's situation any worse than it already is, and he isn't willing to humiliate himself beyond what he's risking now.

Suddenly, there's a loud buzz—the electric lock releasing, signaling him to enter.

The house is cool and silent. Mr. Bradshaw shows Rick into the living room, and it strikes him again how enormous the place is and how far apart the pieces of furniture are. As he takes a seat on the sofa, he wonders if Mr. Bradshaw will be able to hear him from his chair halfway across the cavernous room.

At that moment, Ellen appears. She's dressed in jeans and a dark green blouse that complements her coppery hair. She couldn't look any prettier.

"Hi," Rick says.

"Hi," she replies and sits cross-legged in another big chair.

This is crazy, Rick thinks. *Mr. Bradshaw is treating us as if he'd caught us screwing in the basement.* But he takes a deep breath and tries to speak calmly. "I really, truly didn't mean any harm," he begins. "And I don't think—"

"I can't believe you took Ellen to that slum," cuts in Mr. Bradshaw.

"It's not a slum."

"It's called the barrio," Ellen explains.

"Call it whatever you like," her dad says. "It's not a safe place for an American girl." He speaks calmly, and sitting there in his Hawaiian shirt—this time a red one covered with blue and yellow parrots—he looks relaxed rather than enraged. But Rick finds that no consolation. Mr. Bradshaw doesn't need to raise his voice; he's in control whether he shouts or whispers.

He gazes coolly at Rick. "Then, on top of that, you coerce her into doing stoop labor."

"Daddy, that's not what I said!" Ellen exclaims. She turns at once toward Rick. "I never said I was coerced—honest!—and I never called it stoop labor."

Mr. Bradshaw intervenes. "Well, maybe 'coerce' is too strong. 'Coax'—how about that?"

"I wasn't coaxed. I did it because I wanted to."

Her dad laughs. "Why would anyone want to do such backbreaking work?"

"Because it's *real*!" she shouts. "Because it *matters*!"

"Ellen—"

"It matters a whole lot more than your endless strings of ones and zeros!"

Rick is impressed that Ellen is standing up to her dad, but he's also worried that she'll get them both in deeper trouble. Her last comment seems to have stung Mr. Bradshaw.

He sits forward in his chair. "Is that so?" he asks. "Well, I daresay things don't have to be made of concrete to be real. All those ones and zeros are a lot more substantial than you think."

Rick can see that the conversation is heading into family matters, and he doesn't want it to get sidetracked. "May I say something?" he inquires.

"Go ahead."

"I'm sorry you think getting Ellen involved in the project was a mistake."

"It certainly was."

"I honestly don't believe that Ellen was in any danger—"

"That's not for you to decide."

"—and I never would have asked her to help if I believed she *was* in danger."

"All very comforting," says Mr. Bradshaw.

Ellen looks torn between letting Rick talk and interrupting him. "Dad—"

"The Romeros are good people," Rick continues. "I know them well, and I know their neighbors, and they know me—" Rick isn't finished, but he stops when Mr. Bradshaw raises both hands to silence him.

"Listen to me," Mr. Bradshaw says. "I'm not accusing you of bad intentions. I'm sure you meant well. You're just naive, that's all. It's not that I think someone's going to kidnap Ellen, or that your friends' neighbors will attack her. But you don't understand the risks. If my ex-wife hears that Ellen has been doing manual labor in a poor Mexican neighborhood, she could take me to court."

"Mom wouldn't do that," Ellen states emphatically.

"She might. She could say I'm not attending to your well-being. She could claim I haven't looked after you properly."

"But she can't keep me from spending time with you, Dad. You know that. I'm legally old enough to decide which parent I want to live with, or else both parents."

"True," says Mr. Bradshaw. "But your sisters *aren't* old enough. And because of this—this *incident*—your mother could accuse me of negligence and take me to court. I could lose visitation rights with your sisters."

"No—"

"Yes, Ellen, I really could. Things aren't quite as simple as you imagine."

"Mr. Bradshaw, I won't argue with you," Rick tells him. "Maybe this was a mistake. If so, I'm really, really sorry."

Mr. Bradshaw nods once.

"But I'd like to ask you—can't you give us a little time together? I'll be leaving on the twenty-ninth, and I'd like to spend a few more hours with your daughter."

"I can't go back on what I've told her," he says. "She's grounded."

Ellen gazes at her father with a combination of sorrow and anger, but she says nothing.

"What if she stays here?" he suggests.

"Meaning, you want to visit her in this house?"

"Yes, if you'll let me."

Mr. Bradshaw doesn't answer at first. Finally he says, "I'll think it over."

Pulling Out the Supports

With the *colado* nearly dry, Julio directs Francisco and Rick to remove the *vigas* and *cimbra* that supported it. This is a tricky procedure. They pull out the vertical posts carefully and attempt to remove the horizontal beams without dislodging too many squares of *cimbra* in the process. Most of the time, they're able to proceed without incident. Sometimes a beam falls suddenly once it's unsupported, or else pieces of *cimbra* crash to the floor. Francisco is struck twice by falling *cimbra*. Rick nearly gets hit by a beam.

It's possible, he thinks, *that Julio's injury won't be the last.*

Julio directs the boys as they work and seems impatient with some of their actions. *"Cuidado, ¿eh?"* he cautions. Careful, okay?

"Trataremos," answers Francisco bluntly. We'll try.

"You're not working together."

This comment confirms Rick's impression. He and Francisco are doing the same job at the same time but without coordinating their actions. Often they're at cross-purposes, with one of them removing a support when the other is still in harm's way.

"Please be more careful!" Julio warns them, almost shouting.

Rick half expects him to get involved, to dive into the work despite his injury, but he doesn't. His reluctance tells Rick how much pain he must still be feeling, even though he never speaks of it.

After a few hours, Francisco and Rick have removed all the supports from the *cimbra*. Many of the squares have fallen, but others remain stuck in place. They use crowbars to pull down whatever hasn't come down on its own. The ceilings are corrugated from the imprint of the *cimbra*, and the rooms smell as damp and earthy as the inside of a cave. The *colado* is now unsupported except along the edges.

"Pues, ya lo ves," says Julio. Well, there you have it.

There's a long moment of silence. Rick feels tense. Is it possible

that the whole thing will come crashing down? Despite the solid-
ity of the concrete? Despite the strength of the steel rebar inside?
Is it possible that they messed up somehow, and now the work
will crush the workers? He lets out the breath he's been holding.
No, Ellen was right. It's as solid as a bunker.

"¿Qué piensas, Papi?" Francisco asks.

Julio gazes around, sizing up the work. His face shows the delight of someone admiring a work of art—a magnificent sculpture,
perhaps, or some frescoes on the walls of an ancient church. At last
he says, "Ya es verdaderamente una casa." Now it's truly a house.

Getting Ready

Rick sorts through his belongings. He isn't packing yet—he just
wants to make sure he's got everything he'll need when it's time
to leave. He finds the tourist card he'll surrender on leaving Mexico. The plane ticket he'll use for the flight home. The passport
he'll present on reentering the United States.

Somehow the plane ticket shocks him. 29 AUG, reads the
date. Rick glances at his watch. Today is the twenty-fifth. How
is it possible that his stay here has passed so quickly? At the same
time, his arrival in Mexico feels incalculably distant . . . something
that happened years and years ago. He's been here long enough
to take part in la obra and most of the other tasks necessary for
building the house. Long enough to acquire more Spanish than

in all his years of schooling combined. Long enough to learn new ways to live. Long enough to meet Ellen, fall hard for her, and try to make sense of what they mean to each other.

Rick walks over to the bedroom window and looks out at the patio. Julio is resting in the sun. Emiliana and Hilaria are hanging laundry on the clothesline to dry. Francisco is teasing Tizón and Sombra with a piece of meat—holding it close, then yanking away—prompting them to jump. A radio is playing *música norteña*, jaunty country-western songs from northern Mexico. Out of the kitchen waft rich, spicy odors: roasting peppers, tortillas, beans . . .

What Rick sees and hears and smells is totally different from what he has grown up with, and in many ways his months here have been difficult. Yet he's grown comfortable in this setting, and he feels very close to the Romeros. He's dreading their goodbyes a few days from now. It's going to be hard to leave; this house is now, in its own way, home.

Vete, Gringo

Carrying a stack of *cimbra* on his back, Rick staggers down Callejón Hidalgo. He and Francisco have been hauling beams and wooden squares for the past two hours. With Julio out of commission, it's taking them far longer to carry the materials to the corner than when they lugged the same loads in the opposite direction.

He sees people coming toward him—two guys. He can barely glance up without the risk of tripping. When they pass, one of them says distinctly, *"Vete, gringo."*

Rick almost drops the *cimbra*. Get lost, gringo? He can't believe it. After all he's done to settle into the barrio, to adjust to it, to be part of it! He's seen both guys many times before. He's sure they know he lives with the Romeros. So what's going on?

It's only then that Rick realizes how he has misunderstood his place in this neighborhood. The Romeros welcomed him into their home. They made him part of their family. But Rick has assumed that their acceptance meant that their relatives and neighbors accepted him, too. He's living in the barrio, eating the same kind of food, doing the same kind of work. Surely the people here will treat him as more than just another outsider. Surely they'll admire him for doing things their way. Instead, it's *vete, gringo*. It never occurred to him that his efforts to fit in would meet with amusement, derision, even contempt.

"¡No soy gringo!" he wants to shout. I'm not a gringo! Given a chance, he'll tell them why he's different from the tourists who come to Santo Domingo. He'll describe his parents' longstanding interest in Mexico, his family's friendship with the Romeros, and now his three months in the barrio. He'll make a case that far from being a gringo, he's *casi mexicano*—almost Mexican.

Of course they won't believe him—and why should they? His claim doesn't make sense. The Romeros' neighbors can see Rick living in the barrio, but he doesn't look like them, he doesn't dress like them, he doesn't act like them. Even his rapidly improving Spanish won't persuade them. Everyone knows that he has come from *allá en el norte*. He's here by choice. He can leave when he's ready. He can quit doing this backbreaking work and go back to his easy life in the States. Therefore, he's a gringo.

It's so obvious. The only question is, why did it take him so long to see it?

Lucha Libre

On the twenty-seventh, Rick starts packing his roll-aboard and backpack.

Francisco sits on the sofa and reads a wrestling magazine called *Lucha Libre,* "Free Fight," which has a photo of two fierce-looking, spandex-clad combatants on the cover. He looks up, watches Rick a moment, then says, *"Dos días mas."* Two days to go.

Rick stops short, a folded shirt in his hands. Two days to go. Meaning, "You sure seem eager to leave"? Or meaning, "It's high time you left"?

"I'm just making sure everything fits," he says.

"Vale la pena." That's worth the trouble.

"The airlines are really strict about what they let you take onboard."

"Imagino que sí," Francisco remarks. I imagine so. Then, almost under his breath, he adds, *"Pero, ¿qué sé yo de tales cosas?"* But what do *I* know about such things?

Rick has had enough. "Why are you upset with me?" he asks abruptly.

Francisco goes back to looking at his magazine. "I'm not upset."

"You could have fooled me."

"I'm not upset."

"No?" Rick stares at Francisco, who studiously ignores him. He tells himself to let it go, to keep his mouth shut, but once again he blurts out what's on his mind. "I just don't get it," he says, surprised by how loud his voice sounds. "I come here, I work like a mule, I do my best to help you build your house . . . and you act like I've caused you a lot of problems, like you can't wait for me to leave."

"That's not true." Francisco sets down the magazine and looks at Rick, but Rick can't read his expression.

"Sure seems like it," he says.

"No, that's not true at all."

"Then why are you so—" Rick blanks. How do you say "pissed off" in Spanish?

Before he can go on, Francisco launches into his own tirade. "You think I'm mad because you've caused problems? Well, that's very interesting. Actually, you've *solved* a lot of problems. And I thank you for that, Ricardo. I thank you for everything you've done. First, because I really mean it. And second, because what else can I offer you but my thanks?"

"You don't need to thank me."

"Yes I do."

"Francisco—"

"I know it's not much, after all your work. *And* all the money you've spent. *And* all you've done for my family. But I hope you'll accept it." Francisco's face reddens as he speaks.

Rick is shocked by the suddenness and intensity of their argument. But what hits him even harder is that over these weeks and months he's managed to turn a blind eye to the truth: that his presence may have lifted some of the Romeros' burdens, but it also *created* a burden, in its own way. At least it must feel that way to Francisco.

Rick understands now. He parachutes in, plays a key role in *la obra,* and then escapes. He contributes hundreds of dollars to the effort—money that would have taken Francisco months and months to earn at SuperTienda. He makes a difference to the Romero family in ways that Francisco, despite his deep love for his parents, cannot.

The boys are silent. Francisco resumes reading his magazine. Rick goes back to packing his suitcase. He thinks hard. Maybe there's nothing more to say. But he's determined to try one last time to break the impasse between them, to take their friendship back to where it started.

"I accept your thanks, Francisco. I'm glad I could help," he says. "But here's something . . . something to think about. I've been here three months. Whatever I've done for your family is nothing compared to what you've done in the past. Or what you'll do in the future. And one more thing. If the roles were reversed, you would have done the same for me and my family."

Francisco looks at him a long moment, then nods.

Rick knows he'll have to leave it at that.

Looking for Ellen

When Rick rings the bell at the Bradshaws' house, there's no answer. He rings again. Still no answer. Is Mr. Bradshaw so angry now that he won't even talk with him over the intercom?

Perhaps the family is out; perhaps Rick has just picked the wrong time to stop by. The place looks deserted ... but of course it looks deserted even when it's full of people. He rings the bell again.

The front door opens, and someone emerges. It's the servant who wears the black-and-white waiter outfit. *"¿Sí?"* he says on reaching the gate.

"¿Está la señorita Ellen?" Is Ellen here?

"No está."

"¿Y el señor Bradshaw?"

"No está tampoco." He's not, either.

Discouraged, Rick asks when they will return.

"I don't know, sir."

"This afternoon?"

"Much later. They went to the beach."

"To the *beach?"* Rick is stunned. This is central Mexico; there's no beach closer than a two-day drive. But that's the point, he realizes. Mr. Bradshaw has whisked his daughters away to Manzanillo, Ixtapa, or some other Pacific Coast resort. Who knows, maybe they flew to Cabo San Lucas, at the tip of Baja California, or across the Gulf of Mexico to Cancún. What difference does it make? Any beach resort would be far enough away to keep Rick and Ellen apart, and even a short stay would suffice. Rick had mentioned that he's leaving on the twenty-ninth, so all Mr. Bradshaw has to do is wait two more days.

The servant stands there patiently. His face reveals nothing.

"That's it?" Rick asks. "No message? Did *la señorita* say anything? About me, perhaps?"

Suddenly the man looks uncomfortable. *"No, señor."*

Rick follows a hunch. "Nothing? Are you sure?"

There's a moment's hesitation. "I shouldn't tell you this," the servant says at last, "but she wrote you a letter and asked me to—"

"A letter! Where is it?" Rick is thrilled to hear this news.

"Unfortunately, señor Bradshaw discovered it and took it from me."

"You gave it to him?" His mood plummets again

The servant motions in exasperation. "What was I to do? He's the boss."

"Of course, of course."

"I'm sorry."

"It's not your fault," Rick says. "Thank you for telling me."

He turns and walks off, stunned by what Ellen's father has done in the name of love.

Matters of the Heart

When Rick returns to the Romeros' house, he finds Hilaria sweeping the courtyard with a broom that's taller than she is.

"*¿Por qué estás tan triste, gringuito?*" she asks. Why are you so sad, little gringo?

Rick sighs. If an eight-year-old can figure him out, he hasn't done such a great job hiding his mood. "*Todo está bien,*" he tells her. Everything's fine.

"*No te ves bien.*" You don't *look* fine.

He almost lashes out with *Mind your own business!* But he'd have to be a heartless jerk to brush her off. She looks eager for his company.

"*¿Qué pasó?*" she asks. What happened?

"Oh, nothing much."

"Did you go visit the gringa?"

"I tried to, but she's left town."

"*Qué lástima.*" What a pity. Hilaria looks dejected. "Why did she leave?"

"I don't really know," Rick admits. "I think her father made her go."

"That's too bad."

"True."

Hilaria sets down her broom, and she and Rick sit on the steps. "Isn't it true there are lots more gringas in Gringolandia?" she asks.

"Yes, quite a few," Rick admits.

"So?"

"So what?"

"So—go find yourself another gringa."

"Right," Rick tells her. "I suppose I'll do that."

"Y mientras tanto, yo puedo ser tu novia," Hilaria says cheerily. And in the meantime, *I* can be your girlfriend.

Rick reaches out and hugs her. "Fine. You'll be my girlfriend."

Special Delivery

The doorbell clangs. Rick answers it and finds a messenger with a letter. *Entrega Inmediata* is stamped on the envelope. Special Delivery. No doubt it's from Ellen! She's asking forgiveness for her dad's stupid behavior, explaining what happened, telling him she misses him like crazy. He's about to open the envelope when he notices it isn't addressed to him. It's addressed to Francisco.

"For you," he says, walking down the steps and handing it over.

Francisco tears a strip off the edge of the envelope, slips out a single page, and unfolds it. He reads it once, twice, three times.

Emiliana and Julio come out to the courtyard.

"Pues, ¡habla!" says Emiliana. So, talk!

"¿Qué será?" asks Julio. What is it?

Francisco looks almost faint. "I've been accepted by the teachers' college."

At once there's a great commotion. Emiliana shrieks with delight, Julio cheers, Rick slaps Francisco on the back, Tizón and Sombra bark wildly. Then, as if this racket isn't enough, there's an explosion of wings as all the pigeons in the *pirul* tree take off simultaneously.

What Do You Prefer?

"What is the sea like?" asks Emiliana that evening. Seated in the dim kitchen, they're discussing places they've visited. Rick has traveled much more widely than the Romeros, so he's become the focal point of the conversation.

He fumbles for the right words, trying to describe the size and power of the ocean. Then he says, "I like the sea, but I like the mountains even better. I'm most at home there. In the wilderness, I'm nothing, totally unimportant, but the land makes me feel powerful at the same time."

Julio and Francisco glance at one another. They've listened politely so far, but suddenly they both guffaw.

"Sorry!" Francisco says.

"*¡Tontos! ¡No se rían de Ricardo!*" Emiliana scolds them. You dopes. Don't laugh at Rick! Then she turns to him. "I understand what you're saying. It's a matter of losing your pride, isn't it?"

"I guess so," Rick says, embarrassed by his earlier words.

"That's good," she continues. "That's beautiful. Sometimes at night I gaze at the heavens, and I feel smaller than a bug."

"What kind of bug?" asks Julio in mock seriousness.

"Any kind," replies Emiliana.

"Any?"

"Like I said—I feel just like a bug. Tiny and insignificant before God."

"Reynaldo Beltrán told me about a bug he saw in Chiapas," says Francisco, "down there by the Guatemalan border. A bug you wouldn't believe."

"How big?" asks Julio.

"Big as a mouse!"

"No kidding."

"Big as a small rat!"

"No se burlen de mí," Emiliana warns her family. Don't you mock me.

"Who's mocking?" asks Francisco, pretending not to understand.

It occurs to Rick, just then, why there's so much joking going on. He'll be leaving tomorrow. His departure looms over each conversation he has with the Romeros. Everyone is trying to ignore the obvious.

"I think you know," she tells her son. "But listen, smarty-pants. If you don't like what *I* prefer, tell me what *you* prefer."

Francisco shrugs. "Me? I'm content. I just want to earn my teacher's diploma."

"Well, that's admirable."

"Then maybe I'll get a good job and find myself a wife."

"You're a wonderful son."

Francisco nods, clearly relieved to have passed the test.

"And you, don Julio?" she asks. "What do you prefer?"

"Me?"

"You."

"Riding horses," says Julio with a grin. "Shooting guns, chasing wild animals, catching bad guys. Traveling *al norte* to find good work."

"Ay, don Julio." Emiliana sighs, shaking her head.

A Work in Progress

When he first arrived in Santo Domingo, even before the work started, Rick fantasized about the conclusion of *la obra*. The house would be finished—perfect, complete, with no task left undone. The Romeros would rearrange their belongings and settle in. They'd throw a huge party to celebrate the project's spectacular success—a fiesta complete with hanging lanterns, strolling mariachis, and huge quantities of food. Guests would come from all over the barrio. There might even be fireworks.

Now it's the morning of his departure. In a few hours he'll catch the bus to Mexico City, take a taxi to the airport, and fly home to Denver. His stay is over. The hardest part of *la obra* is over. Yet lots of work remains.

Julio and Francisco will have to plaster the walls and ceilings. They'll string wires from the main line to electrify the house. They'll install windows upstairs and downstairs. They'll build a concrete staircase from the patio to the upper rooms. They'll paint and decorate. Only then will this house truly be finished. So it's appropriate, Rick decides, that there's no party yet.

Later, then. Some other day. Right now it's time to draw this visit to a close.

Gazing from the outermost of the second-floor rooms, Rick can see an almost unbroken panorama of Santo Domingo. The town drops away below the Romeros' hillside property, then spreads out to the right, to the left, and into the desert beyond. Only a few treetops obscure the lower reaches of this view.

The relatively poor dwellings of the Romeros' barrio lie wedged together on the slope. Most resemble what the Romeros own—a small plot of land with walls surrounding a courtyard and a few rooms. Some are larger, some smaller. Some look more affluent than the Romeros'; others look even more humble. Dogs pace inside or stand guard on the flat rooftops. Hens, pigs, goats, and roosters wander about.

Farther down the hillside, the houses are more substantial. Most have stucco walls—some are white, some reddish-brown, some pastel blue, green, or pink. Farther still are the big, beautiful colonial houses, the mansions once owned by Spanish aristocrats and now by Mexican business people and American expatriates.

Rick can't see the mansions in detail, but it's the nearest houses that interest him, anyway. Not just the houses themselves, but their unfinished state: walls half-built, rooms as yet unroofed, gaping holes waiting for doors and windows, piles of building materials stacked in courtyards. Nothing is totally done. Everything is a work in progress. It occurs to Rick that this isn't an aberration; it's the nature of things. It's also how he now feels about this trip, about this stage of his life, about himself.

Suddenly, bells begin to peal. Bells from the cathedral, from every parish church, from every corner chapel. Bells big and little, far and near. Listening, Rick thinks that he has never before heard so many at once. Every single bell in Santo Domingo must be ringing. The din is terrific.

He steps down into the patio. Francisco is playing tug of war with Tizón and Sombre. Hilaria is braiding Emiliana's long black hair. Julio is just resting contentedly in a chair.

"*Pues, ¿qué pasa?* Rick asks.

Everyone seems puzzled by his question.

"*Tantas campanas,*" he explains. So many bells.

Julio gestures in bafflement. "*¡Quién sabe!*" Who knows!

It must be something important, Rick thinks, *a saint's feast day, perhaps, or the commemoration of an event in Christ's life, or a national holiday. One of those.* But for him, the bells of Santo Domingo peal in jubilation and thanksgiving for what he and the Romeros, working together, have accomplished.

IV

Stay in Touch

Arriving home from school one afternoon in late October, Rick checks the mail. It's mostly magazines and bills for his parents. Then he spots an envelope with the red, white, and green striped border of Mexican airmail. It has his name on it! He opens it, but before he can reach in and remove the contents, some photographs and a postcard tumble out.

Rick looks at the postcard first. The picture side shows a view of San Francisco. Addressed to him in care of the Romeros and postmarked Palo Alto, the flip side contains a message in English:

> Rick, I'm sorry things didn't work out better, but there was nothing I could do. Dad thinks I'm still a little girl. Oh well, he'll catch on someday!
>
> Thanks for what you did. I liked the Romeros, and I really enjoyed being part of their project. It's the biggest sculpture I've ever worked on, and I'll never forget it! Tell them hi from la gringa. Love, Ellen

Scribbled in the left margin is Ellen's address and this question: "What colleges are you applying to? Stay in touch."

Rick stares at the postcard for a while, delighted. *Stay in touch . . .*

Then he studies the photos—several views of the Romeros' house. It looks both familiar and dramatically different. The same structure that he helped build, but much less rough-hewn. Windows have been fitted into the window wells. A concrete staircase leads from the courtyard to the second floor. Terra cotta pots with red geraniums decorate the ledge formed by the first-floor roof. Standing near the kitchen door, Julio, Emiliana, and Francisco gaze with pride at the camera.

Rick pulls a letter from the envelope. *"Hola, Ricardo. Pues, ahora puedes ver como hemos terminado la obra . . ."*

> Hi, Ricardo,
>
> Well, now you can see how we've finished the project. It looks very good, and we couldn't be happier with the results. Here are some pictures, plus a postcard that your friend Ellen sent to you at our address.

Francisco goes on to describe the other changes they've made and explains their plans for the future. He also writes about his classes at the teachers' college and brings Rick up to date on his parents and various family members. Rick is pleased to get the news. He's especially glad to hear that Hilaria has convinced Francisco that she should be his first student.

He reads the letter again. He feels very happy—and not simply because the project's late phases have gone so well. At the end of the letter Francisco writes:

> Ricardo, it was wonderful having you here in Santo Domingo. I hope you're as pleased with *la obra* as we are. My parents and I send our thanks

and warmest greetings. Can you come and visit with us again next summer?

Your friend,

Francisco

Pues, ¿cómo no? Rick asks himself. *¡Esto será buenísimo!* Then he notices with amusement that he's thinking in Spanish.

Well, why not? That'll be great!

08/11